INK KNOWS
NO BORDERS

POEMS OF THE IMMIGRANT
AND REFUGEE EXPERIENCE

INK KNOWS NO BORDERS

POEMS OF THE IMMIGRANT AND REFUGEE EXPERIENCE

EDITED BY PATRICE VECCHIONE
AND ALYSSA RAYMOND

SEVEN STORIES PRESS
New York • Oakland • London

A TRIANGLE SQUARE BOOK FOR YOUNG READERS
PUBLISHED BY SEVEN STORIES PRESS

SEVEN STORIES PRESS
140 Watts Street
New York, NY 10013
www.sevenstories.com

College professors and high school and middle school teachers may order free
examination copies of Seven Stories Press titles. To order,
visit www.sevenstories.com or send a fax on
school letterhead to (212) 226-1411.

Book design by Abigail Miller

LIBRARY OF CONGRESS CATALOGING-IN-PUBLICATION DATA

NAMES: Vecchione, Patrice, editor. | Raymond, Alyssa, editor.
TITLE: Ink knows no borders : poems of the immigrant and refugee experience / edited
by Patrice Vecchione and Alyssa Raymond.
DESCRIPTION: New York : Seven Stories Press, [2019] | Audience: Grades 7-8. | "A
Triangle Square Book for young readers." | Includes bibliographical references and
index.
IDENTIFIERS: LCCN 2018052736 (print) | LCCN 2018059209 (ebook) | ISBN
9781609809089 (Ebook) | ISBN 9781609809072 | ISBN
9781609809072 (paperback : alk. paper) | ISBN 9781609809089 (ebook)
SUBJECTS: LCSH: Immigrants—United States—Juvenile poetry. | Refugees—United
States—Juvenile poetry. | American poetry—21st century.
CLASSIFICATION: LCC PS617 (ebook) | LCC PS617.I53 2019 (print) | DDC
811/.60803581—dc 3
LC RECORD AVAILABLE AT https://lccn.loc.gov/2018052736

Printed in the USA.

9 8 7 6 5 4 3 2 1

Contents

To be rooted is perhaps the most important
and least recognized need of the human soul.

—SIMONE WEIL

I wish maps would be without
borders & that we belonged
to no one & to everyone
at once, what a world that
would be.

—YESENIA MONTILLA

let me tell you what a poem brings . . .
it is a way to attain a life without boundaries.

—JUAN FELIPE HERRERA

Editors' Note

At the time of this writing, with the manuscript of *Ink Knows No Borders* nearly complete, the United States is in a dismal mess. Children are separated from their families as they attempt to enter the country, young people who were brought to the US as children without documentation are threatened with deportation, and the Supreme Court has allowed the president to carry out his ban on immigrants based on the idea that some human beings are "illegal."

In his poem "Off-Island Chamorros," Craig Santos Perez writes this truth: "Remember: / home is not simply a house, village, or island; home / is an archipelago of belonging." For people to leave their home and cross a harsh desert or sea, often with small children in tow, they must be fleeing something too difficult for many of us to fully imagine: civil war, political or religious persecution, gang violence, lack of work, hunger, or natural disaster.

Ink Knows No Borders celebrates the lives of immigrants, refugees, exiles, and their families, who have for generations brought their creative spirits, resilience and resourcefulness, determination and hard work, to make this land a home. They have come from the Philippines, Iran, Mexico, Russia, Vietnam, El Salvador, Sudan, Haiti, Syria, you name it. Enter the place of these poems, bordered only by the porousness of paper, and you'll find the world's people striving and thriving on American soil.

There is the daughter whose mother packed three days' worth of underwear in a ziplock bag in case ICE showed up at her school, the child wishing to change her name to something more "American," the dried desert creek where forty people sleep, the beer company that "did not hire Blacks or Puerto Ricans," an immigrant mother's vindication when her math, much to the surprise of fellow shoppers, is proven correct at a check-out counter, a son who "ached to be [as] beautiful" as his praying Muslim father, the fifteen-year-old who understands her parents as poorly as they understand her, the young poet who writes, "I don't know how to think of this— / I wasn't taught to notice one's colors," and more, so much more.

These poets know that the pen holds a secret, a secret that can only be uncovered by putting that pen to paper, in a crowded coffee shop or some solitary place, maybe in the middle of night or when the dawn won't let you sleep, inspired, as you are, by birdsong or your own song. They know that "This story is mine to tell." These lived stories, fire-bright and coal-hot acts of truth telling, are the poet's birthright—and a human right.

Whether you were born in this country or another, whether you came here with the help of a "coyote," crammed in a too-small boat, or with a visa and papers in order, whatever your skin color or first language may be, whomever you love, writing poems is a way to express your most authentic truths, the physical ache of despair, the mountaintop shout of your joy. Writing poetry will help you realize that you are stronger than you thought you were and that within your tenderness is your fortitude.

Not only does ink know no borders; neither does the heart.

PATRICE VECCHIONE and ALYSSA RAYMOND

Foreword

america, am I not your refugee?

—FATIMAH ASGHAR

¿WHEN & HOW can you start to tell the story of where you or your family comes from? ¿The *why* of being in another country? ¿And should you? Growing up in San Rafael, California, after emigrating from El Salvador unaccompanied at the age of nine, I never asked these questions. Didn't dare. From the moment I crossed the border through the Sonoran Desert—no, way before that—from the morning I said goodbye to Grandpa from the back of a bus near the Guatemala–Mexico border, I knew never to speak of what would happen.

I would not see Grandpa for six years, Grandma for nineteen. When I was reunited with my parents, they told me not to tell anyone about being born in another country, about my "illegal entry," about what I had experienced those two months when no one knew my whereabouts, when even the people in my parents' ESL class prayed and lit candles so I would make it here safely. It became my secret. In her poem "Return," Gala Mukomolova writes, "It happens, teachers said, that a child between countries will refuse to speak." Absolutely. Since our reunion in Arizona, I've spoken to my parents about those two months only twice in my life. Both times, after I started writing poetry. Both times, their guilt, their remorse, their asking for forgiveness, made us stop with the questions, and we let out our tears.

Before I had the tools (the pen and paper of poetry) to replay, analyze, revise the trauma my "refugee story" embodied, I held all of that anger deep inside, believing that what I had been through could be forgotten, but trauma doesn't work that way. I thought no one—not my parents, not my friends, not the best counselor—could understand what I had experienced. I truly believed I had been the only nine-year-old who had migrated by himself, crossed an ocean, three countries, and a desert. Like Mahtem Shiferraw describes in her poem "Talks about Race," "I [didn't] know how to fit, adjust myself within new boundaries— / nomads like me have no place as home, no way of belonging." I started drinking and hanging out with the wrong people in my apartment complex. Wearing certain "gang" colors. My friends and I were not real gangsters; we were just trying to prove ourselves to one another. I could've been an honor-roll student in middle school, but my behavior kept me from it. Once, I threw a bottle of water at my seventh-grade teacher. I was kicked out of class multiple times for saying something vulgar to make everyone laugh. I needed to be seen. Heard. I wanted someone to ask me what was wrong with me and truly mean it. For me to be able to break down and cry in front of them. That never happened.

Because I was good at soccer, in part because I let my anger out on the soccer field, I got a fancy scholarship to attend a fancy high school. My first real culture shock. Adjusting to the US after migrating was difficult, but at my elementary and middle schools, everyone looked like me. Not at Branson. I was one of six Latinx students in the entire school of 272. I put up a front. Guarded myself with the baggy clothes, slicked-back hair, gold chain that said "El Salvador," and too much cologne. Even the seniors were scared of me. They'd never seen anyone from my part of Marin County. I continued to act out in class. I wanted to lose my scholarship so I could attend the public high school with my brown friends. Luckily, after the third time I got kicked out of both freshman math and English, I was asked to meet with all my teachers and my soccer coach. They showed me that they really believed in me and gave me an opportunity to succeed. After four years at Branson, I got into UC Berkeley.

It was in high school that I allowed poetry to discover me. My senior-year English teacher devoted a full three weeks to the subject, bringing in a real-life poet, Rebecca Foust, who reintroduced me to Pablo Neruda. My parents owned a CD of *Twenty Love Poems and a Song of Despair* in Spanish, which I hated. But now, seeing Spanish and English on the same page was like magic: the first moment the two sides of my identity existed side by side. And when Neruda talked about the landscape of Chile, his verses reminded me of home. I wrote my first poem "Mi Tierra (My Land)," and began to rediscover what I had tried to forget. Neruda led me to Roque Dalton, Claribel Alegría, Sharon Olds, June Jordan, Yusef Komunyakaa, Charles Simic, and eventually to some poets in this anthology. Poetry showed me that I was not alone. Like Safia Elhillo writes in her poem "self-portrait with no flag," "i pledge[d] allegiance to my / homies." My first real homies—the ones who gave me permission to face my trauma of immigrating, of having left "home"—were poets.

I'd lived a childhood in El Salvador; but like Li-Young Lee says in his poem "A Hymn to Childhood," I just didn't know "which childhood" that had been. ¿Was it one that would "never end," one that I would "never escape"? I knew for certain it was one that "didn't last." It ended too soon. I'd traded hide-and-seek with my friends for real-life hiding from the authorities, in boats, under buses, under bushes. What guided me was the hope of seeing my parents again. That I would finally meet the father that had left me when I was about to turn two. The father who had once held me on his shoulders as he ran on the soccer field before his game. On the page, because of poetry, I could write that reality, those images I'd heard about. I could replay Mom's palms caressing my head before I went to bed.

Poetry let me tap into these and many other memories. It let me tap into everything I've revealed to you now. It has taught me that it's OK to open up. It's OK to look inward, to hold those around us accountable for their actions. Taught me that speaking out is the beginning of healing. I thank my parents for listening to my poems even though the poems were not nice to them. I'm not saying I have completely healed. I'm not saying poetry can fix everything, because it hasn't, but it was the beginning, the constant thing, on my road to my own healing. Like Ocean Vuong writes in his poem "Someday I'll Love Ocean Vuong," "the end of the road is so far ahead / it is already behind us" and "The most beautiful part of your body / is where it's headed." I can see the end now. I can imagine the next step. I know for a fact, I wouldn't be able to do that had poetry not found me. Had I not believed, even for a second, in its magic. I'm writing this at my childhood home in El Salvador, outside with frogs and birds all round. My house is in the flight path from the airport and I remember imagining, as a child, every plane was a plane to the US. Four, five times a day I looked up, seeing the path I hoped to take to be reunited with my parents. It did not occur that way. I did not experience the privilege Lena Khalaf Tuffaha describes in her poem "Immigrant" of leaving my homeland "on the magic carpet of [my] navy blue / US [passport]." I will soon experience that, however. I passed my visa interview and am currently waiting for my passport. It was poetry, not soccer, that got me to college and eventually opened up a path toward an EB-1 visa, a Green Card.

It's been difficult to be here, the place I wanted to return to, but hadn't for nineteen years. Last night I heard gunshots. This morning, the church bells rang, signaling another death. It has been difficult to see how much it has changed, how much I have changed. Like Craig Santos Perez writes in his poem "Off-Island Chamorros," I "feel foreign in [my] own homeland." I've been here three weeks, living in uncertainty, not knowing if I would get approved. All this time children have been separated from their families at the US border. I'm reading and watching the news in the country many of those families are fleeing. It has been a blessing to have the poets you will find in these pages here with me. I'm lucky I can hold these poems close, to show me how to process what I'm living through.

JAVIER ZAMORA

INK KNOWS NO BORDERS

POEMS of the IMMIGRANT and REFUGEE EXPERIENCE

Departure: July 30, 1984

We were not prepared for it—
America, the land cut like a massive slab
of steak. Our mother did not sit us down
to explain, and nothing was said
over the black coffee and rice
soup at mealtimes. My siblings and I approached
our inevitable leaving with numb
acceptance, as people do under martial law.

Days prior to the date, things disappeared
in the house: the display cabinet taken away by an aunt,
the wedding gift china wares in it sold, except for the blue plates
and swan-shaped bowls that would not survive the journey.
The rice bin was given to a family friend; knives
to Uncle Leo; school uniforms, cousins; roosters divided
among the men; floral fabrics for the women; dried
mangoes and stale squid candies for the neighborhood
children; a twin bed transported upstairs
for my sister staying to complete college.

That late July morning, the *jeepney* arrived,
as hired, the sun held dominion over the blinding sky,

a zephyr funneled through the narrowing streets
of Manila. The steady procession of
well-wishers in our house did not halt,
my father handing out *pesos*
as if he was paying for our safe passage.
Surrounded by luggage and boxes huge
as baby elephants, we were each given
a dollar bill, our firsts, as the *jeepney* drove off
to take us to the airport, leaving behind a throng
of onlookers waving violently, and a tearful, older sister
who, years later, would reenact this disappearing act,
this fading scene of a rooster-lined road of this
cockfighting, banana tree-lush town speeding away,
lost in the kinetic gray cement and dark smoke of exhaust.

Joseph O. Legaspi

Immigrant

I am not buckled safely into my seat
I am watching the road unravel
behind us like a ribbon of dust.

Through the back window of my uncle's Datsun
Amman looks like a tender little place
the color of my teddy bear's fur.
Its houses crowded into one another
on its seven parched hills
are the shades of my family's skin—
almond of my mother's brow,
wheat of my father's arms,
tea-with-cream of my grandmother's palms.

We are driving away on the only road to the airport.
We are driving away from this dollhouse town
and my storybook childhood of tree-climbing
and laughter of too many cousins to count.
We are driving away from impending war.

We are driving away
because we can leave

on the magic carpet of our navy blue
US passports that carry us
to safety and no bomb drills
to the place where the planes are made
and the place where the president
will make the call to send the planes
into my storybook childhood
over the seven hills
next door to neighbors who will now
become refugees.

We are driving and I
am not safe
driving away from
myself and everything I know
into the great miracle of
a country so large
wars are kept thousands of miles at bay.
My young life is coming undone
on the road behind me
where I know all the names of
the trees in Arabic
rumman   saru   zayzafoon
and I know the spot on each hilltop
where the crimson poppies return every spring
and I know the best bakery to line up for
Ramadan pancakes before breaking the fast.

In the backseat of my uncle's Datsun
I want to float through the window
and into yesterday
when August was just late-afternoon ice cream

and late-night card games
and the crinkle of brown paper and tape
covering copybooks,
fresh as this morning's bread,
ready to receive the school year ahead—
math equations,
poems,
histories of battle.

Lena Khalaf Tuffaha

First Light

I like to say we left at first light
        with Chairman Mao himself chasing us in a police car,
my father fighting him off with firecrackers,
        even though Mao was already over a decade
dead, & my mother says all my father did
        during the Cultural Revolution was teach math,
which he was not qualified to teach, & swim & sunbathe
        around Piano Island, a place I never read about
in my American textbooks, a place everybody in the family
        says they took me to, & that I loved.
What is it, to remember nothing, of what one loved?
        To have forgotten the faces one first kissed?
They ask if I remember them, the aunts, the uncles,
        & I say *Yes it's coming back,* I say *Of course,*
when it's *No not at all,* because when I last saw them
        I was three, & the China of my first three years
is largely make-believe, my vast invented country,
        my dream before I knew the word "dream,"
my father's martial arts films plus a teaspoon-taste
        of history. I like to say we left at first light,
we had to, my parents had been unmasked as the famous
        kung fu crime-fighting couple of the Southern provinces,

& the Hong Kong mafia was after us. I like to say
        we were helped by a handsome mysterious Northerner,
who turned out himself to be a kung fu master.
        I don't like to say, I don't remember crying.
No embracing in the airport, sobbing. I don't remember
        feeling bad, leaving China.
I like to say we left at first light, we snuck off
        on some secret adventure, while the others were
still sleeping, still blanketed, warm
        in their memories of us.
What do I remember of crying? When my mother slapped me
        for being *dirty, diseased, led astray by Western devils,*
a dirty, bad son, I cried, thirteen, already too old,
        too male for crying. When my father said *Get out,*
never come back, I cried & ran, threw myself into night.
        Then returned, at first light, I don't remember exactly
why, or what exactly came next. One memory claims
        my mother rushed into the pink dawn bright
to see what had happened, reaching toward me with her hands,
        & I wanted to say *No. Don't touch me.*
Another memory insists the front door had simply been left
        unlocked, & I slipped right through, found my room,
my bed, which felt somehow smaller, & fell asleep, for hours,
        before my mother (anybody) seemed to notice.
I'm not certain which is the correct version, but what stays with me
        is the leaving, the cry, the country splintering.
It's been another five years since my mother has seen her sisters,
        her own mother, who recently had a stroke, who has trouble
recalling who, why. *I feel awful,* my mother says,
        not going back at once to see her. But too much is happening here.
Here, she says, as though it's the most difficult,
        least forgivable English word.

What would my mother say, if she were the one writing?
How would her voice sound? Which is really to ask, what is
my best guess, my invented, translated (Chinese-to-English,
English-to-English) mother's voice? She might say:
We left at first light, we had to, the flight was early,
in early spring. *Go*, my mother urged, *what are you doing,
waving at me, crying? Get on that plane before it leaves without you.*
It was spring & I could smell it, despite the sterile glass
& metal of the airport—scent of my mother's just-washed hair,
of the just-born flowers of fields we passed on the car ride over,
how I did not know those flowers were already
memory, how I thought I could smell them, boarding the plane,
the strange tunnel full of their aroma, their names
I once knew, & my mother's long black hair—so impossible now.
Why did I never consider how different spring could smell, feel,
elsewhere? First light, last scent, lost
country. First & deepest severance that should have
prepared me for all others.

Chen Chen

Origin / Adoption

My first mother placed inside my mouth
a thick tongue / a curled tongue
prone to quick rolling music
and bramble-berried consonants
I would never speak to her.
These days, on this other hemisphere
I twist my second mother's words
from my tongue as I do
the fruit from my neighbor's tree:
geu-rhim / *cham-eh* / / fig and yellow
melon arching over the sidewalk,
ripening into dark hills / deep sun.
These days, I peel this craving
already budded with discomfort,
recover utterances too long untouched,
as if I could know the correct
taste of each vowel / inflections
sweet on my fingers and chin.

Marci Calabretta Cancio-Bello

Dear America

You used to creep into my room,
remember?

I was eleven and you kept coming,
night after night, in Tehran, slid in
from inside the old radio on my desk, past
the stack of geometry homework, across
the faded Persian carpet, and thrust
into me, with rock and roll thumps.

I loved you more than bubble gum,
more than the imported bananas
street vendors sold for a fortune.
I thought you were azure, America,
and orange, like the sky, and poppies,
like mother's new dress, and kumquats.

I dreamed of you America, I dreamed
you every single night with the ferocity
of a lost child until you became true like flesh.
And when I arrived at you, you punched
yourself into me like a laugh.

Sholeh Wolpé

Second Attempt Crossing

for Chino

In the middle of that desert that didn't look like sand
        and sand only,
in the middle of those acacias, whiptails, and coyotes, someone yelled
        "¡La Migra!" and everyone ran.
In that dried creek where forty of us slept, we turned to each other,
        and you flew from my side in the dirt.

Black-throated sparrows and dawn
        hitting the tops of mesquites.
Against the herd of legs,

        you sprinted back toward me,
I jumped on your shoulders,
        and we ran from the white trucks, then their guns.

I said, "freeze Chino, ¡pará por favor!"

        So I wouldn't touch their legs that kicked you,
you pushed me under your chest,
        and I've never thanked you.

Beautiful *Chino*—

       the only name I know to call you by—
farewell your tattooed chest: the M,
       the S, the 13. Farewell
the phone number you gave me
       when you went east to Virginia,
and I went west to San Francisco.

       You called twice a month,
then your cousin said the gang you ran from
       in San Salvador
found you in Alexandria. Farewell
       your brown arms that shielded me then,
that shield me now, from La Migra.

Javier Zamora

Bent to the Earth

They had hit Ruben
with the high beams, had blinded
him so that the van
he was driving, full of Mexicans
going to pick tomatoes,
would have to stop. Ruben spun

the van into an irrigation ditch,
spun the five-year-old me awake
to immigration officers,
their batons already out,
already looking for the soft spots on the body,
to my mother being handcuffed
and dragged to a van, to my father
trying to show them our green cards.

They let us go. But Alvaro
was going back.
So was his brother Fernando.
So was their sister Sonia. Their mother
did not escape,
and so was going back. Their father

was somewhere in the field,
and was free. There were no great truths

revealed to me then. No wisdom
given to me by anyone. I was a child
who had seen what a piece of polished wood
could do to a face, who had seen his father
about to lose the one he loved, who had lost
some friends who would never return,
who, later that morning, bent
to the earth and went to work.

Blas Manuel De Luna

A Hymn to Childhood

Childhood? Which childhood?
The one that didn't last?
The one in which you learned to be afraid
of the boarded-up well in the backyard
and the ladder to the attic?

The one presided over by armed men
in ill-fitting uniforms
strolling the streets and alleys,
while loudspeakers declared a new era,
and the house around you grew bigger,
the rooms farther apart, with more and more
people missing?

The photographs whispered to each other
from their frames in the hallway.
The cooking pots said your name
each time you walked past the kitchen.

And you pretended to be dead with your sister
in games of rescue and abandonment.
You learned to lie still so long
the world seemed a play you viewed from the muffled
safety of a wing. Look! In
run the servants screaming, the soldiers shouting,
turning over the furniture,
smashing your mother's china.

Don't fall asleep.
Each act opens with your mother
reading a letter that makes her weep.
Each act closes with your father fallen
into the hands of Pharaoh.

Which childhood? The one that never ends? O you,
still a child, and slow to grow.
Still talking to God and thinking the snow
falling is the sound of God listening,
and winter is the high-ceilinged house
where God measures with one eye
an ocean wave in octaves and minutes,
and counts on many fingers
all the ways a child learns to say *Me*.

Which childhood?
The one from which you'll never escape? You,
so slow to know

what you know and don't know.
Still thinking you hear low song
in the wind in the eaves,
story in your breathing,
grief in the heard dove at evening,
and plentitude in the unseen bird
tolling at morning. Still slow to tell
memory from imagination, heaven
from here and now,
hell from here and now,
death from childhood, and both of them
from dreaming.

Li-Young Lee

Immigrant Aria

there they blow, there they blow, hot wild white breath out of the sea!

—D. H. Lawrence

To swallow new names like krill, dive.
       You have few tides before you
return to motion. Once this shrine

       was the abyssal plain. Once Empire
shackled you. Once you answered
       to monster, to dragon, spewing steam, fire

bellowing in the furnace of your hide,
       a migrant captured for brown skin's
labor. Somewhere inside the darkness

       where brews flame, a spirit hovers
over the deep. Once before Adam named
       you *illegal* you snaked, breaking

into air. Spit out his poison, jaw-clap
        the sea. With your aft-fin's trailing edge
churn surface to milk. In the beginning,

        you were formed with great light.

                                        Rajiv Mohabir

On Being American

You are seven years old when a grown man screams at you, spitting
    knives from crooked purple lips: Go home, fucking Paki.

You are confused because the ethnic slur is inaccurate.

You realize, too young, that racists fail geography but that their
    epithets and perverted patriotism can still shatter moments of
    your childhood.

You are the last to know that everyone else sees you as Other.

You keep your eyes on your paper and study and do well and stay quiet
    and obey.

You get patted on the head and told you're one of the good ones.

You are a model.

Until you aren't.

Because those manners you once minded and that tongue you once bit
    won't be held back anymore.

Can't be.

And what they think is rebellion is, in truth, survival. Because if you
　　　stay silent one second longer, the anger surging through your
　　　blood will engulf you in flames.

So you snatch their words from the air:
Terrorist
Rag head
Sand nigger
And burn them like kindling and rub the embers onto your skin, a
　　　sacrilege, a benediction, a qurbani.

For the girl you once were.
For the girl you are becoming.

The one who doesn't ask to be recognized,
But demands to be known.

The one who presses into her fears to speak out. To stand up. To live.
　　　Anything else is death.

The one who learns that sometimes the enemy is a smiling neighbor too
　　　ashamed to reveal herself except behind the dark curtain of the
　　　ballot box. Sometimes your enemy is a friend.

You are tired of fighting for your name. And tired of the eternal
　　　question: Where are you really from?

You persist.

Because your name is who you are.

You weep.

For a land built on the backs of your black and brown brothers and
sisters and soaked in their blood.

You claim your joy.

You lay your roots:

Blood and bone and fire and ash.

And in this land of the free and home of the brave, you plant yourself.

Like a flag.

Samira Ahmed

Oklahoma

For a place I hate, I invoke you often. Stockholm's: I am eight years old and the telephone poles are down, the power plant at the edge of town spitting electricity. Before the pickup trucks, the strip malls, dirt beaten by Cherokee feet. *Osiyo, tsilugi.* Rope swung from mule to tent to man, tornadoes came, the wind rearranged the face of the land like a chessboard. This was before the gold rush, the greed of engines, before white men pressing against brown women, nailing crosses by the river, before the slow songs of cotton plantations, the hymns toward God, the murdered dangling like earrings. Under a redwood, two men signed away the land and in history class I don't understand why a boy whispers *sand monkey.* The Mexican girls let me sit with them as long as I braid their hair, my fingers dipping into that wet black silk. I try to imitate them at home—*mírame, mama*—but my mother yells at me, says they didn't come here so I could speak some beggar language. Heaven is a long weekend. Heaven is a tornado siren canceling school. Heaven is pressed in a pleather booth at the Olive Garden, sipping Pepsi between my gapped teeth, listening to my father mispronounce his meal.

Hala Alyan

On Listening to Your Teacher Take Attendance

Breathe deep even if it means you wrinkle
your nose from the fake-lemon antiseptic

of the mopped floors and wiped-down
doorknobs. The freshly soaped necks

and armpits. Your teacher means well,
even if he butchers your name like

he has a bloody sausage casing stuck
between his teeth, handprints

on his white, sloppy apron. And when
everyone turns around to check out

your face, no need to flush red and warm.
Just picture all the eyes as if your classroom

is one big scallop with its dozens of icy blues
and you will remember that winter your family

took you to the China Sea and you sank

your face in it to gaze at baby clams and sea stars

the size of your outstretched hand. And when
all those necks start to crane, try not to forget

someone once lathered their bodies, once patted them
dry with a fluffy towel after a bath, set out their clothes

for the first day of school. Think of their pencil cases
from third grade, full of sharp pencils, a pink pearl eraser.

Think of their handheld pencil sharpener and its tiny blade.

Aimee Nezhukumatathil

The Break-In

When I close my eyes I see my mother running
from one house to another, throwing her fist
at the doors of neighbors, begging anyone
to call the police.
There are times when every spectator is hungry,
times a thief takes nothing, leaves you a fool
in your inventory.
How one trespass could make all others
suddenly visible. My mother counted
her jewelry and called
overseas. My father counted women
afraid one of us would go
missing. When I close my eyes
I hear my mother saying, "*A'aha*, this new country,"
my cousins exclaiming "Auntie!"
between the clicking line and their tongues.
Tonight the distance between me, my mother, and Nigeria
is like a jaw splashed against a wall.
I close my eyes and see my father
sulking like a pile of ashes,
his hair jet black and kinky,
his silence entering a thousand rooms.

Then outside, trimming hedges as if home
were a land just beyond the meadow,
the leaves suddenly back.
When I close my eyes
I see my mother, mean for the rest of the day,
rawing my back in the tub
like she's still doing dishes.

Hafizah Geter

#Sanctuary

The grownups keep saying to be calm and donate to animals
but the storms in my heart are too loud, even if they help you
evolve, Ma says, so for an energy filter I meditate with my iPod

but as soon as someone insists my cleverness is the cause of my anxiety
I want to tell them RELAX is not the same as BE STUPID—
since Friday a dozen people got shot and is it safe

for illegals? Ma believes in love, gratitude, laughter, cupids and candles.
Every time I tell her I can't cope with the stress, she refers to music.
To me sanctuary is physical, has a body, teeth that can be

kicked in. Ma says I need to get some spirit, we can talk about it
in 15 more minutes. When Angel disappeared, it was his car
registration sticker expired. I can't believe they call the lockup

ICE. When I say nobody but Native Americans really comes from here
the boy at school says the United States became the greatest thing
that ever happened to the world, even if not everybody

gets to benefit from the rules. He yells, Before we were immigrants
at least we were conquerors! My parents argued when Da found out

how much money Ma gave the elephant fund, while my little sister's

busy drawing turkey hands and getting in the way. That kid was born here
amongst the conquerors and I bet she marries one. Then I'll remind her
I am not a flood and nobody opened the gates for me. Now Ma is giving

a dollar to send "Nosey" to a real sanctuary because somebody hooked him
to a trailer weighing more than a ton. I too am a draft horse whose hoofs
need shoes, whose soul is not waterproof, whose energy center leaks,

whose refuge is not horizontal not black & white, more like dawn
rolling over me from grey into a hundred shards of roses hand-painted
in my scared dreams. Sometimes I love how Ma stirs the chili pot

and watches a kangaroo on YouTube. When I say, Ma we need to talk
about a Sanctuary City, she says, Hey isn't that the name of a cosmetics
center in Arlington? Her motto is "Never microwave anything

you care about." I'll save it for my children; but also, "We Are People
Not Preventable Crimes" and "I am a Mini-Donation to Everyone I Know!"
Now that the world is in turmoil, my motto is "Like a raptor

I fall on my enemies with ferocity, because I am kind."

JoAnn Balingit

Extended Stay America

My mother ran me across
the school quad, swearing

they would come for me
first. In a bag ziplocked

right to left across my lap
she had filled and Pentel-penned

three days worth of underwear
and a cordless telephone

from Pick 'n Save.
I could smell the manure

and saddle leather as we drove
down the 60.

She told me they wouldn't
hesitate to lug me

by the back of my shirt,

to drag me over the front

yard like a bundle
of firewood. I cracked

the window, left shoe marks
on the motel sheets.

High on Astro Pops
and candy cigarettes,

she said, *Now
your classmates will know.*

Janine Joseph

Choi Jeong Min

For my parents, Choi Inyeong & Nam Songeun

in the first grade i asked my mother permission
to go by frances at school. at seven years old,

i already knew the exhaustion of hearing my name
butchered by hammerhead tongues. already knew

to let my salty gook name drag behind me
in the sand, safely out of sight. in fourth grade

i wanted to be a writer & worried
about how to escape my surname—choi

is nothing if not korean, if not garlic breath,
if not seaweed & sesame & food stamps

during the lean years—could i go by f.j.c.? could i be
paper thin & raceless? dust jacket & coffee stain,

boneless rumor smoldering behind the curtain
& speaking through an ink-stained puppet?

my father ran through all his possible rechristenings—

ian, isaac, ivan—and we laughed at each one,

knowing his accent would always give him away.
you can hear the pride in my mother's voice

when she answers the phone *this is grace*, & it is
some kind of strange grace she's spun herself,

some lightning made of chain mail. grace is not
her pseudonym, though everyone in my family is a poet.

these are the shields for the names we speak in the dark
to remember our darkness. savage death rites

we still practice in the new world. myths we whisper
to each other to keep warm. my korean name

is the star my mother cooks into the jjigae
to follow home when i am lost, which is always

in this gray country, this violent foster home
whose streets are paved with shame, this factory yard

riddled with bullies ready to steal your skin
& sell it back to your mother for profit,

land where they stuff our throats with soil
& accuse us of gluttony when we learn to swallow it.

i confess. i am greedy. i think i deserve to be seen
for what i am: a boundless, burning wick.

a minor chord. i confess: if someone has looked
at my crooked spine and called it elmwood,

i've accepted. if someone has loved me more
for my gook name, for my saint name,

for my good vocabulary & bad joints,
i've welcomed them into this house.

i've cooked them each a meal with a star singing
at the bottom of the bowl, a secret ingredient

to follow home when we are lost:
sunflower oil, blood sausage, a name

given by your dead grandfather who eventually
forgot everything he'd touched. i promise:

i'll never stop stealing back what's mine.
i promise: i won't forget again.

Franny Choi

Muslim Girlhood

I never found myself in any pink aisle. There was no box for me
with glossy cellophane like heat and a neat packet of instructions
in six languages. Evenings, I watched TV like a religion
I moderately believed. I watched to see how the others lived, not
          knowing
I was the Other, no laugh track in my living room, no tidy and
          punctual
resolution waiting. I took tests in which Jane and William had
so many apples, but never a friend named Khadija. I fasted
through birthday parties and Christmas parties and ate leftover *tajine*
at plastic lunch tables, picked at pepperoni from slices like blemishes
and tried not to complain. I prayed at the wrong times in the wrong
tongue. I hungered for Jell-O and Starbursts and margarine, could read
mono- and diglycerides by five and knew what *gelatin* meant, where it
          came from.
When I asked for anything good, like Cedar Point or slumber parties,
I offered a quick *Inshallah*, as in *Can Jordan sleep over this weekend,*
          Inshallah?,
peeking at my father as if he were a god. Sometimes, I thought
my father was a god, I loved him that much. And the news thought
this was an impossible thing—a Muslim girl who loved her father.
But what did they know of my heart, or my father

who drove fifty miles to buy me a doll like a Barbie
because it looked like me, short brown hair underneath her hijab,
    unthreatening
breasts and feet flat enough to carry her as far as she wanted
to go? In my games, she traveled and didn't marry, devoured any book
she could curl her small, rigid fingers around. I called her *Amira*
because it was a name like my sister's, though I think her name
was supposed to be *Sara*, that drawled *A* so like *sorry*,
which she never, ever was.

Leila Chatti

Fluency

The once-monthly obligation was the phone,
a plastic conch shoved into her young palm,
static ocean carrying her English
over eight time zones to Borneo and reaching

this aunt or another with a name plucked
from the Bible, changed by accent,
laughter not needing translation
as it surfaced. She imagined this

as her mother's revenge for supermarket corrections
on pronunciation, throat now clotted
with the tangled seaweed of words
made meaningless. She can't blame her

for the relishing of this silence.
In the end, the girl would flee, the instrument
surrendered and an outheld hand
putting things back where they ought to be.

Michelle Brittan Rosado

Master Film

my mother around that blue porcelain,
my mother nannying around the boxed grits and just-add-water pantry
of the third richest family in Alabama,
my mother at school on Presbyterian dime and me
on my great grandmother's lap singing
her home, my mother mostly gone
and elsewhere and wondering
about my dad, my baba, driving a cab
in Poughkeepsie, lifting lumber in Rochester, thirtysomething
and pages of albums killed,
entire rows of classrooms
disappeared, my baba drowning Bud Light by the Hudson
and listening to "Fast Car," my baba on VHS
interviewed by a friend in New York, his hair
black as mine is now, I'm four and in Alabama, I see him
between odd jobs in different states,
and on the video our friend shows baba a picture
of me and asks *how do you feel when you see Solmaz?*
and baba saying *turn the camera off* then

turn off the camera and then
can you please look away I don't want you to see my baba cry

Solmaz Sharif

The Key

I was under the kitchen table, guessing who was at the sink by how they used water when I heard my mother say to my father, what about this job, that one, those people, did they call? And my father said, everyone says no. I see all the doors but none of them will open. My mother said, maybe we just haven't found the right key, I'll go look for it. They laughed for a long time. Their toes looked at each other. Maybe they forgot the bag of keys in the crooked-mouth dresser. I lined up the keys on a windowsill, metal on metal on my fingers until they smelled like missing teeth. I looked at the best one: large cursive *F*, a scarlet ribbon tied to it. It had two teeth, like my baby sister. I tried the little door behind the community center. Then the big-kids door at my school. The shed of a house with a backyard so large the family could never see me. I got grass and sand and an ignorant pebble in my shoe. Dust climbed up my pants so I could spit-spell my name on my leg when resting. I went back to our neighborhood. There was a black cloud over it while the nice neighborhood down the hill shone. A girl said our house was darkest and the first raindrops fell on it because we're all going to hell. When I told my father he said it was "isolated" or "separated" storms. So it was true we were set apart for a punishment. The next day dozens of dead flying ants covered our patio. I took all the keys and tried all the doors in the abandoned mall. One unlocked. It was a room with white walls, floor, ceiling. White squares of wood flat or leaning in every corner. The door closed behind me and no key would work. Maybe the room would swallow me and I'd get invisible if I didn't stop screaming but then a surprised guy, white, wearing white, opened the door. I wanted to try one more time but my keys disappeared and everyone said they were never real.

Ladan Osman

Ode to the Heart

heart let me more have pity on

—Gerard Manley Hopkins

It's late in the day and the old school's deserted
but the door's unlocked. The linoleum dips
and bulges, the halls have shrunk.
And I shiver for the child
who entered that brick building,
his small face looking out
from the hood of a woolen coat.

My father told me that when he was a boy
the Jews lived on one block, Italians another.
To get home he had to pass
through the forbidden territory.
He undid his belt and swung it wildly
as he ran, wind whistling
through the buckle. Heart
be praised: you wake every morning.
You cast yourself into the streets.

Ellen Bass

The Sign in My Father's Hands

for Frank Espada

The beer company
did not hire Blacks or Puerto Ricans,
so my father joined the picket line
at the Schaefer Beer Pavilion, New York World's Fair,
amid the crowds glaring with canine hostility.
But the cops brandished nightsticks
and handcuffs to protect the beer,
and my father disappeared.

In 1964, I had never tasted beer,
and no one told me about the picket signs
torn in two by the cops of brewery.
I knew what dead was: dead was a cat
overrun with parasites and dumped
in the hallway incinerator.
I knew my father was dead.
I went mute and filmy-eyed, the slow boy
who did not hear the question in school.
I sat studying his framed photograph
like a mirror, my darker face.

Days later, he appeared in the doorway

grinning with his gilded tooth.
Not dead, though I would come to learn
that sometimes Puerto Ricans die
in jail, with bruises no one can explain
swelling their eyes shut.
I would learn too that "boycott"
is not a boy's haircut,
that I could sketch a picket line
on the blank side of a leaflet.

That day my father returned
from the netherworld
easily as riding the elevator to apartment 14-F,
and the brewery cops could only watch
in drunken disappointment.
I searched my father's hands
for a sign of the miracle.

Martín Espada

History Lesson

My grandfather left school at fourteen
to work odd jobs until he was old enough
to join his Lithuanian kin chipping
anthracite out of the Pennsylvania hills.
Nine hours a day with five hundred feet
of rock over his head, then an hour's
ride home on the company bus
to a dinner of boiled cabbage and chicken.
When the second big war broke
he headed "sout," as he pronounced it,
for better work in the blast furnaces
churning out steel along the shores
of the Chesapeake. Thirty-two years
and half an index finger later he retired
to a brick rancher he built with his own hands
just outside the Baltimore city line.
The spring he got cancer and I got a BA
from a private college we stood under
a tree in his backyard while he copped
a smoke out of my grandmother's sight.
"Tell me, Pop," I said, wanting to strike up
a conversation, "how did you like

working in the mills all those years?"
He studied my neatly pressed white shirt,
took a long drag on his cigarette and spit a fleck
of tobacco near my shoes. "*Like*," he said,
"didn't have a thing to do with it."

Jeff Coomer

My Father Takes to the Road

My father, who never owned a new car,
brings a used one home every Friday
from Tom Lawson's Used Buick.
He takes me along for a test drive,
and I admire the almost new
tuck-and-roll and cherry paint job.
"Are you gonna buy it?" I ask,
forgetting last week's disappointment,
the station wagon with the fold-down seat,
which fit my seven-year-old body.
"We'll see," he coos, teasingly.
Still dressed in his work clothes,
he drives ever so slowly
down the dirt road that divides
the strawberry fields, trying not
to stir up the dust.
I laugh when he steers with no hands.
He points the car west
toward the ocean, the same one
he crossed on a steamer at thirteen,
leaving behind an island boyhood
of bare feet, a bamboo hut with floorboards

you could see through.
He doesn't have to say anything. I already know.
I know my father, who, after a hard day's work,
relishes this drive which must come to an end:
before the hired braceros
return to the bunkhouse
and break into song;
before the hot smell of flour tortillas
permeates the air; before my seven
brothers and sisters are bathed;
before Mr Kralj, the Slavonian landlord,
arrives in his Ford pick-up
to pick up his share,
his half of the week's profit.
My father, who pushes back the car seat
and unlaces his boots, who will not buy
this car today or any other, is trying
to bear down on the wheel,
is steering with his wide brown feet.

Jeff Tagami

My Grandmother Washes Her Feet
in the Sink of the Bathroom at Sears

My grandmother puts her feet in the sink
      of the bathroom at Sears
to wash them in the ritual washing for prayer,
wudu,
because she has to pray in the store or miss
the mandatory prayer time for Muslims
She does it with great poise, balancing
herself with one plump matronly arm
against the automated hot-air hand dryer,
after having removed her support knee-highs
and laid them aside, folded in thirds,
and given me her purse and her packages to hold
so she can accomplish this august ritual
and get back to the ritual of shopping for housewares

Respectable Sears matrons shake their heads and frown
as they notice what my grandmother is doing,
an affront to American porcelain,
a contamination of American Standards
by something foreign and unhygienic
requiring civic action and possible use of disinfectant spray

They fluster about and flutter their hands and I can see
a clash of civilizations brewing in the Sears bathroom

My grandmother, though she speaks no English,
catches their meaning and her look in the mirror says,
I have washed my feet over Iznik tile in Istanbul
with water from the world's ancient irrigation systems
I have washed my feet in the bathhouses of Damascus
over painted bowls imported from China
among the best families of Aleppo
And if you Americans knew anything
about civilization and cleanliness,
you'd make wider washbasins, anyway
My grandmother knows one culture—the right one,

as do these matrons of the Middle West. For them,
my grandmother might as well have been squatting
in the mud over a rusty tin in vaguely tropical squalor,
Mexican or Middle Eastern, it doesn't matter which,
when she lifts her well-groomed foot and puts it over the edge.
"You can't do that," one of the women protests,
turning to me, "Tell her she can't do that."
"We wash our feet five times a day,"
my grandmother declares hotly in Arabic.
"My feet are cleaner than their sink.
Worried about their sink, are they? I
should worry about my feet!"
My grandmother nudges me, "Go on, tell them."

Standing between the door and the mirror, I can see
at multiple angles, my grandmother and the other shoppers,
all of them decent and goodhearted women, diligent

in cleanliness, grooming, and decorum
Even now my grandmother, not to be rushed,
is delicately drying her pumps with tissues from her purse
For my grandmother always wears well-turned pumps
that match her purse, I think in case someone
from one of the best families of Aleppo
should run into her—here, in front of the Kenmore display

I smile at the midwestern women
as if my grandmother has just said something lovely about
    them
and shrug at my grandmother as if they
had just apologized through me
No one is fooled, but I

hold the door open for everyone
and we all emerge on the sales floor
and lose ourselves in the great common ground
of housewares on markdown.

Mohja Kahf

Frank's Nursery and Crafts

The lines are long and my mom insists
that the final amount is wrong.
The cashier looks at the receipt and insists that it's right.
My mom purses her lips, looks worried,
says, *it's not right.*
The line of white people behind us groans.
My mom won't look back at them.
We both know what they're thinking.
Small woman with no knowledge of the way
things are in America.
Though year after year
she makes flowers bloom in the hood,
petals in the face of this land
that doesn't want her here.
Finally a manager comes, checks, and tells the cashier
she rang up twenty-two plants instead of just two,
overcharging us by forty dollars.

My mother holds my hand,
leads me away
without looking back
at the line of white people
who overhear
and gasp,
their sympathy won.
If only I was old enough
to tell them to keep it;
it's not my mom's English
that is broken.

Bao Phi

In Colorado My Father Scoured
and Stacked Dishes

in a Tex-Mex restaurant. His co-workers,
unable to utter his name, renamed him Jalapeño.

If I ask for a goldfish, he spits a glob of phlegm
into a jar of water. The silver letters

on his black belt spell *Sangrón*. Once, borracho,
at dinner, he said: Jesus wasn't a snowman.

Arriba Durango. Arriba Orizaba. Packed
into a car trunk, he was smuggled into the States.

Frijolero. Greaser. In Tucson he branded
cattle. He slept in a stable. The horse blankets

oddly fragrant: wood smoke, lilac. He's an illegal.
I'm an Illegal-American. Once, in a grove

of saguaro, at dusk, I slept next to him. I woke
with his thumb in my mouth. ¿No qué no

tronabas, pistolita? He learned English
by listening to the radio. The first four words

he memorized: In God We Trust. The fifth:
Percolate. Again and again I borrow his clothes.

He calls me Scarecrow. In Oregon he picked apples.
Braeburn. Jonagold. Cameo. Nightly,

to entertain his cuates, around a campfire,
he strummed a guitarra, sang corridos. Arriba

Durango. Arriba Orizaba. Packed into
a car trunk, he was smuggled into the States.

Greaser. Beaner. Once, borracho, at breakfast,
he said: The heart can only be broken

once, like a window. ¡No mames! His favorite
belt buckle: an águila perched on a nopal.

If he laughs out loud, his hands tremble.
Bugs Bunny wants to deport him. César Chávez

wants to deport him. When I walk through
the desert, I wear his shirt. The gaze of the moon

stitches the buttons of his shirt to my skin.
The snake hisses. The snake is torn.

Eduardo C. Corral

Learning to Pray

My father moved patiently
cupping his hands beneath his chin,
    kneeling on a janamaz

                then pressing his forehead to a circle
                    of Karbala clay. Occasionally
                he'd glance over at my clumsy mirroring,

    my too-big Packers T-shirt
and pebble-red shorts,
    and smile a little, despite himself.

                Bending there with his whole form
                    marbled in light, he looked like
            a photograph of a famous ghost.

    I ached to be so beautiful.
I hardly knew anything yet—
    not the boiling point of water

or the capital of Iran,
            not the five pillars of Islam
or the Verse of the Sword—

    I knew only that I wanted
to be like him,
        that twilit stripe of father

            mesmerizing as the bluewhite Iznik tile
                hanging in our kitchen, worshipped
            as the long faultless tongue of God.

                        Kaveh Akbar

Naturalization

His tongue shorn, father confuses
snacks for *snakes, kitchen* for *chicken*.
It is 1992. Weekends, we paw at cheap
silverware at yard sales. I am told by mother
to keep our telephone number close,
my beaded coin purse closer. I do this.
The years are slow to pass, heavy footed.
Because the visits are frequent, we memorize
shame's numbing stench. I nurse nosebleeds,
run up and down stairways, chew the wind.
Such were the times. All of us nearsighted.
Grandmother prays for fortune
to keep us around and on a short leash.
The new country is ill fitting, lined
with cheap polyester, soiled at the sleeves.

Jenny Xie

East Mountain View

Found in a dumpster: folding table, can of Pringles. Half full,
    half empty: it doesn't matter. Perspective's no good

to the stomach, which, unlike the mind, is indentured by habit,
    by imperative. Blame evolution. Blame the gods

from which we absorb our preference for dominion, mimicking
    what we misinterpret as power unaccompanied

by consequence. This is how we become new Americans:
    five-finger discount, Midas touch. Transfiguration

as anti-assimilation, my mother fashions dining set and dinner
    with the loot she lugs into our apartment while I,

months old, not even potty-trained, dream of cities shorn
    and shores away, where a daughter barters her mother's

last gold bangle for guaranteed passage out of the Mekong Delta,
    where a daughter barters the last thing she owns:

her body, her crow-black hair parted down the middle,
  the length of nights lost in the South China Sea,

nights she relives whenever their faceless forms, like sudden
  lightning, surprise her in the flesh of ordinary things—

the coyotes, the pirates, the virgins vaulting into bottomless dark,
  nourishing sharks and not their captors. I suppose

that's survival: to appropriate what annihilates us, to make use
  of what appears useless. I know this despite what it took

to know it. I know this despite the conceit of knowing. It sucks
  belonging to anywhere, to anything. Even in Heaven

we're trespassers, told we don't speak English well enough.
  Even in Heaven we apply for citizenship and wait.

Heaven's a lot of waiting. So we master the grief of geography,
  severed from a life that persists as shadows of shadows.

Paul Tran

Acolyte

The white cross pales
further still,
      nailed arms
watchful as window-light

furls over the backs
of our knees,
      as lavender shadows
cut off our little

necks. I am an infidel
in this classroom
      church. I kneel with
the other, restless

on the cracked leather
kneeler. I crave these
      pillars of candle.
My mouth is avid; it

sings *fidelis, fidelis.*
My maa is in her
        kitchen crooning
black-and-white film

songs that curl her
hennaed fingers
        around the rolling pin's
heavy back and forth.

My baba leans forward
in his chair, the Qur'an
        open to the last
page, the dark words

blurring as his eyes close
to reconcile again the shapla-
        shaped epitaph
on his father's tombstone.

With my head bowed,
I whisper, "Amar naam
        Tarfia," until it is
a prayer that grows.

I help stack the hymnals
higher; I cup the candle
        away. I cry out, "Bismillah!"
before I disrobe.

Tarfia Faizullah

Tater Tot Hot-Dish

The year my family discovered finger food
recipes, they replaced the roast duck with a turkey,
the rice became a platter of cheese and crackers,
none of us complained. We all hated the way the fish
sauce made our breath smell. When the women
started lightening their hair, we blamed it on the sun.
When Emily showed up with blonde highlights
and an ivory boyfriend, we all started talking
about mixed babies. Overjoyed with the possibility
of blue eyes in the family photo. That year
I started misspelling my last name, started reshaping
myself to have a more phonetic face. Vietnam
became a place our family pitied, a thirsty rat
with hair too dark and a scowl too thick.
We stopped going to temple and found ourselves
a church. That year my mother closed her eyes
and bowed her head to prayers she couldn't understand.

Hieu Minh Nguyen

Pronounced

You excavate anything that has tried to lodge itself
in your body without permission. You bury the toothbrush
against your right molar and scrape and scrape whatever

you find. Loss makes you feel all the other losses.
Eleven years later when you no longer eat pizza
or speak Spanish, when your father's silhouette invades

your clenched jawline, you borrow his brisk gait,
his snort, his face. People say you look white.
Your father never does. The restaurant won't seat

you. The hostess says neither of you meet dress
code (your father wearing a double-breasted suit).
You are a man trying to roll your *r*'s. Where did

they go? You are still trying to excavate the sounds
you once dreamt in. You hardly remember your mother
tongue. You are trying to pull something useable from

the wreckage. It all feels familiar. Your best friend
compliments your clean pronunciation. The way you have
learned to let go of everything you once called home.

Carlos Andrés Gómez

Off-Island Chamorros

My family migrated to California when I was 15 years old.
During the first day at my new high school, the homeroom
teacher asked me where I was from. "The Mariana Islands,"
I answered. He replied: "I've never heard of that place.
Prove it exists." And when I stepped in front of the world map
on the wall, it transformed into a mirror: the Pacific Ocean,
like my body, was split in two and flayed to the margins. I
found Australia, then the Philippines, then Japan. I pointed
to an empty space between them and said: "I'm from this
invisible archipelago." Everyone laughed. And even though
I descend from oceanic navigators, I felt so lost, shipwrecked

on the coast of a strange continent. "Are you a citizen?"
he probed. "Yes. My island, Guam, is a U.S. territory."
We attend American schools, eat American food, listen
to American music, watch American movies and television,
play American sports, learn American history, dream
American dreams, and die in American wars. "You
speak English well," he proclaimed, "with almost no
accent." And isn't that what it means to be a diasporic
Chamorro: to feel *foreign in a domestic sense.*

Over the last 50 years, Chamorros have migrated to
escape the violent memories of war; to seek jobs, schools,
hospitals, adventure, and love; but most of all, we've migrated
for military service, deployed and stationed to bases around
the world. According to the 2010 census, 44,000 Chamorros
live in California, 15,000 in Washington, 10,000 in Texas,
7,000 in Hawaii, and 70,000 more in every other state
and even Puerto Rico. We are the most "geographically
dispersed" Pacific Islander population within the United
States, and off-island Chamorros now outnumber
our on-island kin, with generations having been born
away from our ancestral homelands, including my daughter.

Some of us will be able to return home for holidays, weddings,
and funerals; others won't be able to afford the expensive plane
ticket to the Western Pacific. Years and even decades might pass
between trips, and each visit will feel too short. We'll lose contact
with family and friends, and the island will continue to change
until it becomes unfamiliar to us. And isn't that, too, what it means
to be a diasporic Chamorro: to feel foreign in your own homeland.

And there'll be times when we'll feel adrift, without itinerary
or destination. We'll wonder: What if we stayed? What if we return?
When the undertow of these questions begins pulling you
out to sea, remember: migration flows through our blood
like the aerial roots of i trongkon nunu. Remember: our ancestors
taught us how to carry our culture in the canoes of our bodies.
Remember: our people, scattered like stars, form new constellations
when we gather. Remember: home is not simply a house,
village, or island; home is an archipelago of belonging.

Craig Santos Perez

A New National Anthem

The truth is, I've never cared for the National
Anthem. If you think about it, it's not a good
song. Too high for most of us with "the rockets'
red glare" and then there are the bombs.
(Always, always there is war and bombs.)
Once, I sang it at homecoming and threw
even the tenacious high school band off key.
But the song didn't mean anything, just a call
to the field, something to get through before
the pummeling of youth. And what of the stanzas
we never sing, the third that mentions "no refuge
could save the hireling and the slave"? Perhaps
the truth is every song of this country
has an unsung third stanza, something brutal
snaking underneath us as we blindly sing
the high notes with a beer sloshing in the stands
hoping our team wins. Don't get me wrong, I do
like the flag, how it undulates in the wind
like water, elemental, and best when it's humbled,
brought to its knees, clung to by someone who
has lost everything, when it's not a weapon,
when it flickers, when it folds up so perfectly

you can keep it until it's needed, until you can
love it again, until the song in your mouth feels
like sustenance, a song where the notes are sung
by even the ageless woods, the shortgrass plains,
the Red River Gorge, the fistful of land left
unpoisoned, that song that's our birthright,
that's sung in silence when it's too hard to go on,
that sounds like someone's rough fingers weaving
into another's, that sounds like a match being lit
in an endless cave, the song that says my bones
are your bones, and your bones are my bones,
and isn't that enough?

Ada Limón

Portrait of Isako in Wartime

Ohio, and I imagine her
   walking the train line,
tracks narrowed in the distance.
   Through her soles,
the platform's slats. She feels
   their unevenness
in the flats of her feet. Noon-
   day heat and the wool
of her jacket's itchy.
   She's got a bob, it's 1943
and the war's on. No one
   in the station looks
like her, but everyone's
   looking at her.
No explanation but the one
   in government-issued print.
National Student Relocation
   Council. *Early Release.*

The sentry in his watch-
           tower, barbed-wire fence
and Stars and Stripes flapping
           in the wind. From across
the tracks, a man (here,
           imagination does the work
history's lost) approaches, finger
           bared, a blunt accusation.
Aren't you a *Jap*? The long
           explanation—why she's out,
whose side she's on.
           The nations we pledge
at odds, leaving us to make
           up the difference.
This story's old, the woman
           —dead, papers boxed
in a back closet. I've seen them.
           Early Release.
The government-issued ID number.

           In camp, it's said, they cut
gardens into Arkansas desert,
           fixed rocks into the flat face
of the earth and irrigated
           bean rows to feed their families.
Healthy vines appeared
           where none should have

grown; tiny buds coaxed
      from the earth, tendrils
that spooled runners
      through dust.
When the order came
      to pack up and return
home, the authorities found
      every curtain drawn
shut. Every barrack
      floor swept clean.

Mia Ayumi Malhotra

Domesticity

In Chinese, the word *country* is half
the word *home*: 家. Written before a name,
家 also means *domesticized*, as in daughter

whittling her ribs into toothpicks.
Daughter breaking clean
as a bowl. I grow full on

steam. I eat through all my leashes, swallow
a sky twice my size. I gather rust
between my fingers, my girlhood

grown out of. In this country, I choose
between living like an animal or dying
like one. Be the tongueless dog or the hunger

it was rescued from. There is nothing alive
about me. I prove it with a passport
photo of my birth: my mother unknotting

me from a length of rope. Someday
a child will slip out of my body
like a neck from a noose. Motherhood

an attempt at my own life. I envy birds
who fly domestic, their bodies
native to the same sky. Our wings

are alien, attached backwards, angled
wounds. Instead of flight, we learned
butchery. How best to eat from

our injuries. We blow on our cuts
like cooling soup. Serve me
in a corset, a country waisting me

so thin I double as a blade. My birth
certificate an x-ray. The doctor
counts my bones, naming each

a way he can break me. There is nothing
meat about me. I am all joint, all
hinge. My body opens

no doors. To enter a country, leave
me behind. Water your garden
with gunshot. What grows is a woman

stemless, seedless. I am always ready

for bite, for arrow. I am always ready
to run. How else does an animal

learn distance
as dying. How else do I
learn home

is my hunter.

Kristin Chang

The Poet at Fifteen

after Larry Levis

You wear faded black
and paint your face white as the blessed
teeth of Jesus
because brown isn't high art
unless you are a beautiful savage.

All the useless tautologies—

This is me. I am this. I am me.

In your ragged
Salvation Army sweaters, in your brilliant

awkwardness. White dresses
like Emily Dickinson.

I dreaded that first Robin,
so, at fifteen you slash
your wrists.

You're not allowed
to shave your legs in the hospital.

The atmosphere
that year: sometimes you exist
and sometimes you think you're Mrs. Dalloway.

This is bold—existing.

You do not understand your parents
who understand you less:
your father who listens to ABBA after work,
your mother who eats expired food.

How do you explain what you have done?
With your hybrid mouth, a split tongue.

How do you explain the warmth
sucking you open, leaving you
like a gutted machine?

It is a luxury to tell a story.

How do you explain
that the words are made by more
than your wanting?

Te chingas o te jodes.

At times when you speak Spanish, your tongue
is flaccid inside your rotten mouth:

disgraciada, sin vergüenza.

At the hospital they're calling your name
with an accent on the *E*. They bring you
tacos, a tiny golden crucifix.

Your father has run
all the way from the factory.

Erika L. Sánchez

Someday I'll Love Ocean Vuong

Ocean, don't be afraid.
The end of the road is so far ahead
it is already behind us.
Don't worry. Your father is only your father
until one of you forgets. Like how the spine
won't remember its wings
no matter how many times our knees
kiss the pavement. Ocean,
are you listening? The most beautiful part
of your body is wherever
your mother's shadow falls.
Here's the house with childhood
whittled down to a single red trip wire.
Don't worry. Just call it *horizon*
& you'll never reach it.
Here's today. Jump. I promise it's not
a lifeboat. Here's the man
whose arms are wide enough to gather
your leaving. & here the moment,
just after the lights go out, when you can still see
the faint torch between his legs.
How you use it again & again

to find your own hands.
You asked for a second chance
& are given a mouth to empty out of.
Don't be afraid, the gunfire
is only the sound of people
trying to live a little longer
& failing. Ocean. Ocean—
get up. The most beautiful part of your body
is where it's headed. & remember,
loneliness is still time spent
with the world. Here's
the room with everyone in it.
Your dead friends passing
through you like wind
through a wind chime. Here's a desk
with the gimp leg & a brick
to make it last. Yes, here's a room
so warm & blood-close,
I swear, you will wake—
& mistake these walls
for skin.

Ocean Vuong

ode to the first white girl i ever loved

it was kindergarten
& i did not know english
so i could not talk
without being ridiculed

& the teacher did not want me in her class
she was white, too
she said i do not know
how to teach someone
who only speaks spanish

& the kids did not want me in their class
they were white, too
they said we do not know
how to be friends with someone
who only speaks spanish

& i was the only Mexican
& i only spoke spanish
i watched a lot of tv
& everyone was rich & white
my family was poor & Mexican

my family only spoke spanish

& in school i felt so lonely
my loneliness would walk home with me
my loneliness held my hand as i crossed streets
my loneliness spoke spanish like my family

& this is how i learned to equate
my family with loneliness
how i learned to hate my family
how i learned to hate being Mexican

& i watched a lot of tv
& everyone was rich & white
& what i wanted was to grow up
& be rich & white & speak english
on shows like Seinfeld or Friends
on shows with laughtracks, big hair, & cardigans

& what i wanted was friends
to walk home from school with me
& what i wanted was a teacher
to give me gold stars like the other kids
& what i wanted was to stop eating welfare nachos
with government cheese

& it was kindergarten
& i loved all the white girls in my class
Robin & Crystal & Jen & all of the white girls
whose names i've forgotten

i wanted to kiss them

i thought kisses were magic
& i hoped i could learn english through a kiss
that i could run my hands through their hair
& find a proper accent

i loved white girls
as much as i hated
being lonely & Mexican

lord, i am a 25 year old man
& sometimes still a 5 year old boy
& i love black women & latina women

& i tell them in spanish
how beautiful they are
& they are more beautiful & lovely
than all the white women in the world

i tell them in spanish
how lonely it is to live in english
& they answer with a remix of my name
    yo se, yo se, yo se

José Olivarez

Talks about Race

I have dark skin, dark face, and darkened eyes—

the white resides only outside the pupil.

I don't know how to think of this—
I wasn't taught to notice one's colors;

under the sun, everyone's skin bounces streaks of light.

Which do I claim? It is difficult to explain
the difference between African & African American
the details escape me, thin paper folding the involucre of a burning fire.

I am "other"; it is such
an indistinguishable form, beyond the construct of the proper self.

Sometimes I am asked
if I am Indian, Middle Eastern, or Biracial;

I don't know what to say to these people
who notice the shape of the eye before its depth
the sound of the tongue before its wisdom
the openness of a palm before its reach.

And what to those who call me "African"?
Don't they know I can count the years spent back home
wishing I knew I was "African"?

And how to cradle and contain the disappointment that is
rekindled whenever someone does NOT know
my Ethiopia, my Eritrea.

I don't know how to fit, adjust myself within new boundaries—
nomads like me have no place as home, no way of belonging.

Mahtem Shiferraw

Mama

I was walking down the street when a man stopped me
and said,
Hey yo sistah, you from the motherland?
Because my skin is a shade too deep not to have come from foreign soil
Because this garment on my head screams Africa
Because my body is a beacon calling everybody to come flock to the
    motherland
I said, *I'm Sudanese, why?*
He says, *'cause you got a little bit of flavor in you,*
I'm just admiring what your mama gave you

Let me tell you something about my mama
She can reduce a man to tattered flesh
without so much as blinking
Her words fester beneath your skin and the whole time,
You won't be able to stop cradling her eyes.
My mama is a woman, flawless and formidable in the same step.

Woman walks into a war zone and has warriors
cowering at her feet
My mama carries all of us in her body,

on her face, in her blood
And blood is no good once you let it loose
So she always holds us close.

When I was 7, my mama cradled bullets in the billows of her robes.
That same night, she taught me how to get gunpowder out of cotton
    with a bar of soap.
Years later when the soldiers held her at gunpoint
and asked her who she was
She said, *I am a daughter of Adam, I am a woman, who the hell are you?*

The last time we went home, we watched our village burn,
Soldiers pouring blood from civilian skulls
As if they too could turn water into wine.
They stole the ground beneath our feet.

The woman who raised me
turned and said, *don't be scared*
I'm your mother, I'm here, I won't let them through.
My mama gave me conviction.
Women like her
Inherit tired eyes,
Bruised wrists and titanium-plated spines.
The daughters of widows wearing the wings of amputees
Carry countries between their shoulder blades.

I'm not saying dating is a first-world problem, but these trifling
    motherfuckers seem to be.
The kind who'll quote Rumi, but not know what he sacrificed for war.
Who'll fawn over Lupita, but turn their racial filters on.
Who'll take their politics with a latte when I take mine with tear gas.

Every guy I meet wants to be my introduction to the dark side,
Wants me to open up this obsidian skin and let them read every tearful
    page,
Because what survivor hasn't had her struggle made spectacle?

Don't talk about the motherland unless you know
that being from Africa means waking up an afterthought
in this country.
Don't talk about my flavor unless you know
that my flavor is insurrection, it is rebellion, resistance
My flavor is mutiny
It is burden, it is grit, and it is compromise
And you don't know compromise until you've rebuilt your home for
    the third time
Without bricks, without mortar, without any other option

I turned to the man and said,
My mother and I can't walk the streets alone
back home anymore.
Back home, there are no streets to walk anymore.

Emtithal Mahmoud

Split

I see my mother, at thirteen,
in a village so small
it's never given a name.

Monsoon season drying up—
steam lifting in full-bodied waves.
She chops bắp chuối for the hogs.

Her hair dips to the small of her back
as if smeared in black
and polished to a shine.

She wears a deep side-part
that splits her hair
into two uneven planes.

They come to watch her:
Americans, Marines, just boys,
eighteen or nineteen.

With scissor-fingers,
they snip the air,
point at their helmets

and then at her hair.
All they want is a small lock—
something for a bit of good luck.

Days later, my mother
is sent to the city
for safekeeping.

She will return home once,
only to be given away
to my father.

In the pictures,
the cake is sweet
and round.

My mother's hair
which spans the length
of her áo dài

is long, washed, and uncut.

Cathy Linh Che

When the Man at the Party Said
He Wanted to Own a Filipino

When the man at the party told me that he'd always
wanted his very own Filipino, I should've said,
all I've ever wanted was my very own 70-year-old

white man (which is what he was), but I didn't say
that, because it wasn't true. Instead, I said nothing,
but I almost said, amicably: Yes, our bodies are banging,

aren't they? Our skin is leather upholstery beneath
the savage sun, our eyes are fruits fallen from the highest
trees, the bottoms of our unshod feet the color

of amethyst. I almost said: We will parade around
your living room in a linen cloth and feed you turtle eggs
and Cornioles meat from a porcelain dish. I almost said:

I'll be your Filipino, you be my Viking. We'll ride in
a boat together. I'll wear your horny helmet. But I said
nothing. At that party, I wanted to be liked, which is

my tragic flaw. I always find myself on the street smiling
at people who look to be Neo-Nazis. I call it a "safety
smile." Rarely do they smile back, but I would hug them

if they needed it, if I think it would spare me. I used to
wonder if this amenability was inherited. Raja Humabon,
a Filipino king in the 1500s, did not resist Magellan's

missionary agenda. Humabon greeted Magellan and his
Christian lord with friendship. Maybe out of genuine
religious feeling, or maybe servitude and friendship are a type

of fire-retardant, protected from the torches that burned
down the villages of the chiefs who refused to kneel. Of course,
there were some who refused to kneel, and maybe this is

also something inherited too, along with everything else,
all the possible variations, and it doesn't take me long to
realize the flaws in this notion of an inherited friendliness.

When I was thirteen or fourteen, the white husband
of my parents' friend showed me pictures of his Filipino
wife in different bikinis, the ones she sent him in letters

before he hopped on a plane to the Philippines to marry her.
He had a 5x7 album full of these photographs, these early
flirtations. It made him nostalgic to sift through them.

What's good about my wife, he said, is that she's easy
on the eyes. A tuft of his chest hair appeared from the collar
in his shirt, and the soul inside of me nearly choked on its

own regurgitations. Before I could ask if he'd sent her
pictures of himself, I heard his wife's bright cackle from
the other room, like the firing of artillery from a distant ship.

I noted that she was not easy on the ears, that she was not
easy at all. I realize now that this story was never about us
being owned, because we will always own ourselves. This story

is about the way the world believes that it owns us, holding
its album of pictures in its wishful hands. And we are not
amenable as much as we are insidious. We are the Cornioles,

who, after being eaten alive by a whale, enters the whale's body
and takes small, tender bites of the whale's enormous heart.

Marianne Chan

Ode to Enclaves

My lineage is Little Saigon
        asphalt, three generations
                under one roof and mother-

land recipes. On Saturdays,
        my family congregates
                at our favorite restaurant:

Kim Phuong. Here, we worship
        the hot pot; stuff our bellies
                with blessings. My auntie says—

If we're gonna suffer,
        we gotta do it over good food.
                The pavement's cracked

but we know what to do. After
        all, these are neighborhoods of necessity.
                I remember

the first time I saw white faces
        descend upon Little Saigon,
                their crooked beaks eager to pick

meat off these streets. Squawking
        about craft beers and raw
                denim, their foreign tongues

butcher every name on the menu.
        All their Yelp reviews sound the same—
                "I discovered a real gem in Little Saigon.

So authentic! I give it 4 stars.
        Would have been 5, but the waitress
                could have smiled more."

Now, *Kim Phuong* has a 30-minute wait,
        plays Radiohead instead of Khánh Ly
                ballads. Waitresses speak enough English

to accommodate vegan diets.
        Food bloggers all praise the tabernacle
                of my childhood, beg to know the magic

of my people. In the 1800s,
        riots ignited violence against Chinese
                immigrants. After finding refuge

in each other, they kindled new homes:
        Chinatowns. Haven't Asian American enclaves
                always been neighborhoods of necessity?

Before my people built this Little Saigon,
        white flight to the suburbs sucked
                this city's economy down to its marrow.

But we know how to take leftovers
        and forge something beautiful. Funny
                how this city would be boneyard

without us. Now white folks flock
        back to the streets they deserted;
                rediscover everything we rebuilt.

Of course we learned how to be digestible,
        how to shove our limbs into takeout boxes,
                skin ourselves and sell the flesh

for profit. The owners of *Kim Phuong*
        can pay off debt, send their daughter to college.
                When their restaurant burns down

one winter night, they do not cry.
        They can afford to rebuild everything.
                In Vietnamese, *Kim Phuong* means golden

phoenix. I don't say this for the irony.
        It's not this poem's punchline, but my people's
                expectation that everything ours can burn

at any second. Koreatown, Little India,
        Banglatown, Little Manila—no matter
                how many pick at the bones

of immigrant communities,
      we always endure the scorch
           and cackle with a smile.

These neighborhoods of necessity,
      always demanding we cook up
           the most authentic kind

of survival: After all,
      if we're gonna suffer,
           we gotta do it over good food.

Chrysanthemum Tran

Ethnic Studies

In college, I sit in the back with all of the other students of color
and listen as our white peers theorize the hell
out of the oppression that we were born from.
Buzzwords like   institutionalized racism   class warfare
are sugar on their tongues—sweet and comfortable:
words from a language my community
doesn't even know exists because we're too busy
living the realities of them.

It's one thing to major in Ethnic Studies,
it's another to be the reason
for its existence.
For the white students in my major,
Ethnic Studies is like a free study abroad program
that doesn't require that they bring their baggage with them.
A privilege that is easy for them to close in their textbook
at the end of class.

But study my racial profile until
it exhausts you.
Study how Black looks a lot like
the green light for "stop   and frisk."

How Brown has been made
to look like a much-needed check stop
for any given border. Ask me
what it's like to have your skin be made to
feel like the nuclear missile we all know
is coming.
And you still won't know how to sit in the back of a class
and be studied because of how tragic your history is,
as if we weren't brought in to be dissected,
as if Frogs, Rats and People of Color
can only be understood when you cut them open.

When ethnics study Ethnic Studies   it's not school anymore.
It's a lesson in survival.
And I'm tired of playing teacher with my oppression.
If I'm not doing it on a stage, I'm doing it from the margins of a classroom.
I'm doing it from the margins in my notebook.
Always on the margin of something   never the core.
Never asked to be more than what makes me easy
to feel sorry for.

It's easy to avoid confronting the things that make us
uncomfortable. The things that make us feel guilty.
Who chooses to walk through the warzone
if you were told that you don't have to?
If you grew up believing that there isn't one?
If what you don't know won't kill you?
Race is the rent I pay for this skin.
But the belief that racism doesn't exist anymore
is when I feel the foreclosure of this home   taking my knees
from right under me.
You can't claim that racism doesn't exist

when you've never known what it means to survive it.
When you keep looking at the warzone like a teaching moment
you're not ready to learn the lesson from.
A comfort zone you're not willing to sacrifice.

It's easy to avoid confronting the things that make us
uncomfortable. The things that make us feel guilty.
But comfort is what kills us in the long run.
Comfort is sitting down when you should be on your feet.
    It's staying quiet when you should be speaking up.
        It's speaking too much, when you should be listening.
           It's putting up borders for safety, and not
           bridges for healing.
             Comfort is celebrating diversity, but
             never discussing it.
As if a black president is enough.
As if a heritage month is enough.
As if Ethnic Studies is enough.
As if this poem is enough.

Comfort is sitting in the front of the class
forgetting   that we're sitting right behind you.
Wanting to tell you that the warzone still exists.
Wanting to tell you that
this isn't comfortable
for any of us.

Terisa Siagatonu

The Day I Realized We Were Black

my brother Hector was four hours late coming home from work
when he entered the house   He was angry I was holding his pet
rabbit in my arms watching The Godfather—which part I can't remember
did I mention he was angry   sixteen and angry

and he said his legs ached like what the wind must feel against a
tumbleweed
and he said he was tired like death seemed easy like rice and beans
and whatever meat we had that night was too hard to swallow
and he said he wished we were white
and I stood up startled my much lighter skin than his
could not wrap my coarse hair around the idea that we were not that

because my mother is Cuban with grey eyes
because my father had an afro once but I had not noticed then
because my grandfather once said "I wish I were King Kong so I could
          destroy Harlem and those fucking black cockroaches"
because my godparents were Irish-American
because I had suppressed my blackness
because my brother shook me when I told him he was stupid   we were Latino
because he had missed his Jersey to Port Authority bus
because he was walking to the nearest train station and lost his way

because he was stopped by the police
because he was hit with a stick
because he was never given the right directions even though he begged
because trash was thrown at him from the police cruiser's window as he walked
because he was never the same
because we're black
because we're black and I never knew   I was twenty-two

Yesenia Montilla

quaking conversation

i want to talk about haiti.
how the earth had to break
the island's spine to wake
the world up to her screaming.

how this post-earthquake crisis
is not natural
or supernatural.
i want to talk about disasters.

how men make them
with embargoes, exploitation,
stigma, sabotage, scalding
debt and cold shoulders.

talk centuries
of political corruption
so commonplace
it's lukewarm, tap.

talk january 1, 1804
and how it shed life.

talk 1937
and how it bled death.

talk 1964. 1986. 1991. 2004. 2008.
how history is the word
that makes today
uneven, possible.

talk new orleans,
palestine, sri lanka,
the bronx and other points
of connection.

talk resilience and miracles.
how haitian elders sing in time
to their grumbling bellies
and stubborn hearts.

how after weeks under the rubble,
a baby is pulled out,
awake, dehydrated, adorable, telling
stories with old-soul eyes.

how many more are still
buried, breathing, praying and waiting?
intact despite the veil of fear and dust
coating their bruised faces?

i want to talk about our irreversible dead.
the artists, the activists, the spiritual leaders,
the family members, the friends, the merchants,
the outcasts, the cons.

all of them, my newest ancestors.
all of them, hovering now,
watching our collective response,
keeping score, making bets.

i want to talk about money.
how one man's recession might be
another man's unachievable reality.
how unfair that is.

how i see a haitian woman's face
every time i look down at a hot meal,
slip into my bed, take a sip of water,
show mercy to a mirror.

how if my parents had made different
decisions three decades ago,
it could have been my arm
sticking out of a mass grave.

i want to talk about gratitude.
i want to talk about compassion.
i want to talk about respect.
how even the desperate deserve it.

how haitians sometimes greet each other
with the two words "honor"
and "respect."
how we all should follow suit.

try every time you hear the word "victim,"
you think "honor."

try every time you hear the tag "john doe,"
you shout "respect!"

because my people have names.
because my people have nerve.
because my people are
your people in disguise.

i want to talk about haiti.
i always talk about haiti.
my mouth quaking with her love,
complexity, honor and respect.

come sit, come stand, come
cry with me. talk.
there's much to say.
walk. much more to do.

Lenelle Moïse

Atlantis

Whenever I talk about Dominican-Haitian relations
I'm told, you, daughter of Manhattan,
of a multitude of diasporas,
what know you of this island?

What I know is simple:
The island of my people
has twin saltwater lakes,
one   on the side of Haiti,
the other, in the Dominican Republic.
They are three miles apart,
and for the last ten years,
they've both been rising.

What I know is simple:
This island is a history of tangled tresses
I struggle to comb through.
This island, the first wound in the western world.
This island, the first place to undo its locks.
This island, strips people stateless,
stakes them to the wrong side of a cross,
pushes them to a borderland between lakes.

This island, split discs at the mountain spine.

What I know is simple:
Even when the nations misremember,
the land is older. The water is older.
Lake Enriquillo and Laz Azuei
have both been rising, like twin sisters
unpressing themselves from the mud,
stretching up and out
fingering the fields that
once held yucca, and sugarcane;
drowning crops, embalming them in salt.

What I know is this is an unprecedented event.
These two bodies of water
reaching towards each other
as if they've forgotten to whom they owe patriotism.
Or maybe it's simply that they've remembered,
that sometimes the only way to get family to wade in the water,
is to extend to them this unholy baptism.

Elizabeth Acevedo

The Border: A Double Sonnet

The border is a line that birds cannot see.

The border is a beautiful piece of paper folded carelessly in half.

The border is where flint first met steel, starting a century of fires.

The border is a belt that is too tight, holding things up but making it
hard to breathe.

The border is a rusted hinge that does not bend.

The border is the blood clot in the river's vein.

The border says *Stop* to the wind, but the wind speaks another
language, and keeps going.

The border is a brand, the "Double-X" of barbed wire scarred into the
skin of so many.

The border has always been a welcome stopping place but is now a Stop
sign, always red.

The border is a jump rope still there even after the game is finished.

The border is a real crack in an imaginary dam.

The border used to be an actual place but now it is the act of a
thousand imaginations.

The border, the word *border*, sounds like *order*, but in this place they do
not rhyme.

The border is a handshake that becomes a squeezing contest.

The border smells like cars at noon and woodsmoke in the evening.

The border is the place between the two pages in a book where the
      spine is bent too far.
The border is two men in love with the same woman.
The border is an equation in search of an equals sign.
The border is the location of the factory where lightning and thunder
      are made.
The border is "NoNo" the Clown, who can't make anyone laugh.
The border is a locked door that has been promoted.
The border is a moat but without a castle on either side.
The border has become Checkpoint *Chale*.
The border is a place of plans constantly broken and repaired and
      broken.
The border is mighty, but even the parting of the seas created a path,
      not a barrier.
The border is a big, neat, clean, clear black line on a map that does not
      exist.
The border is the line in new bifocals: below, small things get bigger;
      above, nothing changes.
The border is a skunk with a white line down its back.

                                                    Alberto Ríos

Las Casas Across Nations

These houses raised me,
teaching me to see the world through bifocals:

The house on Brooklyn,
where we defrosted the Thanksgiving turkey for mole
by throwing it up and down the stairs.

In the Buena Vista Migrant Camp,
a man fried eggs on his motor every morning.
There, at eight years old, I was the only licensed childcare provider.

The house on Privada de Volantín
gave me a kiss when I was twelve
that has lasted a lifetime.
There, among the other miracles of my life,
I learned that jello can survive outside the fridge.

Near the owner's house, in the apple orchards,
I learned to cover my mouth before dirt
made it its property.

In Ciudad Juárez, my mother made water

and food out of sand, with only her love
and a transistor radio.

On Juan N. Zubirán, where our house
was lower down than the rest,
I learned that dignity
is carried mostly by the neck.

In El Rancho, in Mexico,
I learned to kill a pig with a knitting needle
by going for his heart,
and in Chicago, I learned that a pig can kill you.

At Campus Road in LA, in Ray Otero's sociology class,
I learned success is not about "The Color Game,"
but whether or not you have a car.

At 22 Sudden, in Watsonville, children
were having children,
desperate to birth the fruit
of their parents' wishes.

On Bronte, in California, I sang to pray, and sang to eat,
and sang to drink a better part of myself,
while Mamá began to die through her breast,
that monument all its own, that container of pesticides
from the broccoli, cauliflower, apples,
strawberries, blackberries,
and peaches eaten on the line.

Gabriella Gutiérrez y Muhs

Mexicans Begin Jogging

At the factory I worked
In the fleck of rubber, under the press
Of an oven yellow with flame,
Until the border patrol opened
Their vans and my boss waved for us to run.
"Over the fence, Soto," he shouted,
And I shouted that I was American.
"No time for lies," he said, and pressed
A dollar in my palm, hurrying me
Through the back door.

Since I was on his time, I ran
And became the wag to a short tail of Mexicans—
Ran past the amazed crowds that lined

The street and blurred like photographs, in rain.
I ran from that industrial road to the soft
Houses where people paled at the turn of an autumn sky.
What could I do but yell *vivas*
To baseball, milkshakes, and those sociologists
Who would clock me
As I jog into the next century
On the power of a great, silly grin.

Gary Soto

Field Guide Ending in a Deportation

I confess to you my inadequacies. I want to tell you things I do not know about myself. I've made promises to people whom I will never see again. I've cried in an airport bathroom stall in El Paso, TX when immigration denied my father's application. It felt like a mathematical equation—everything on one side needed to equal everything on the other. It almost made sense to be that sad. I am not compelled to complicate this metaphor. I'm selling this for two dollars. Years ago, on my birthday, I came out to my friends. I thought about the possibility of painting their portraits. What a stupid idea. I've started to cover up certain words with Barbie stickers in my journal. It occurs to me, sitting in my car, at a Dollar General parking lot, in search of cheap balloons for a party which I do not care about, that I am allowed my own joy. I pick the brightest balloons, pay, drive home and dress for the party. I mouth the words *happy birthday to you* in a dark room lit by everyone's phone cameras. Afterwards, I enter all of my emails from five years into a cloud engine and the most used word is *ok*. I confess that I have had a good life. I spend many nights obsessing over the placement of my furniture. I give you my boredom. I give you my obligation. I give you the night I danced and danced and danced at a child's birthday party, drunk and by myself. I've been someone else's shame. It's true, at its core, amá was deported because she was hit by a car. For years to come, this will be the ending of a sad joke she likes to tell. I laugh each time she tells the joke to strangers. Something about how there is more metal than bone in her arm. Something about a magnet. She says *I thought I had died and death meant repeating a name forever.* She says *el jardin encierra la boca de mis pasos.* But this is a bad translation. It's more like *I felt like a star, I felt like somebody famous.*

Marcelo Hernandez Castillo

I Used to Be Much Much Darker

I used to be
much much darker
dark as la tierra
recién llovida
and dark was all
I ever wanted:
dark tropical
mountains
dark daring
eyes
dark tender lips
and I would sing
dark
dream dark
talk only dark

happiness
was to spend
whole
afternoons
tirado como foca
bajo el sol

"you're already
so dark
muy prieto
too indio!"
some would lash
at my happy
darkness but
I could only
smile back

now I'm not as
dark as I once was
quizás sean
los años
maybe I'm too
far up north
not enough sun
not enough time
but anyway
up here "dark"
is only for
the ashes
the stuff
lonely nights
are made of

Francisco X. Alarcón

A Habitable Grief

Long ago
I was a child in a strange country:

I was Irish in England.

I learned
a second language there
which has stood me in good stead:

the lingua franca of a lost land.

A dialect in which
what had never been could still be found:

that infinite horizon. Always far
and impossible. That contrary passion
to be whole.

This is what language is:
a habitable grief. A turn of speech
for the everyday and ordinary abrasion
of losses such as this:

which hurts
just enough to be a scar.

And heals just enough to be a nation.

Eavan Boland

Return

There are poets with history and poets without history, Tsvetsaeva claimed, living through the ruin of Russia.

Karina says *disavow* every time I see her. We, the daughters between countries, wear our mean mothers like scarves around our necks.

Every visit, mine recounts all the wrongs done against her

ring sent for polishing returned with a lesser diamond, Y*ears of never rest and*, she looks at me, *of nothing to be proud.*

I am covered in welts and empty pockets so large sobs escape me in the backroom of my landlord's fabric shop. He moves to wipe my tears

as if I'm his daughter or
I'm no one's daughter.

It's true, I let him take my hand, I am a girl who needs something. I slow cook bone grief, use a weak voice.

My mother calls me *the girl with holes in her hands* every time I lose something.

All Russian daughters were snowflakes once, and in their hair a ribbon long
as their body knotted and knotted and knotted into a large translucent bow.

It happens, teachers said, that a child between countries will refuse to speak.
A girl with a hole in her throat, every day I opened the translation book.

Silent, I took my shoes off when I came home,
I put my house clothes on.

We had no songs, few rituals. On Yom Kippur, we lit a candle for the dead
and no one knew a prayer.

We kept the candle lit, that's all.

The wave always returns, and always returns a different wave.
I was small. I built a self outside my self because a child needs shelter.

Not even you knew I was strange.
I ate the food my family ate, I answered to my name.

Gala Mukomolova

Adrift

The little river
with soft ripples
sent me adrift
to a rudderless life—
no anchor.

My hometown
remote but alive
here on my tongue.

Could I go home again
where poetry nurtured me?
Would the little river
receive me back to its flow?

Alice Tao

Author's Prayer

If I speak for the dead, I must leave
this animal of my body,

I must write the same poem over and over,
for an empty page is the white flag of their surrender.

If I speak for them, I must walk on the edge
of myself, I must live as a blind man

who runs through rooms without
touching the furniture.

Yes, I live. I can cross the streets asking "What year is it?"
I can dance in my sleep and laugh

in front of the mirror.
Even sleep is a prayer, Lord,

I will praise your madness, and
in a language not mine, speak

of music that wakes us, music
in which we move. For whatever I say

is a kind of petition, and the darkest
days must I praise.

Ilya Kaminsky

Game Of Thrones

If this is how I get my family back
then let me have it. My land of water
-fall & mountains before the parking
lot full of dead corpses. Put me back

in a time where I could fight.
When fighting was more than poring
over books, trying to teach myself
the ghost of my mother's tongue

from youtube videos. If we're talking
about dreams then let me be honest.
I call for my family each night
in this borrowed tongue, in this language

not mine but which I wield daily.
Where is my blood-memory? Why
can't my stone eggs hatch once touched?
Am I not my own kind of magic?

Let me speak Saraiki without being taught.
Bring me to a time when I could touch steel
& wilt a man's flesh for coming after my home.

When I could touch the hem of my daadi

ama's lengha as she looked out of the window
& whispered, *the blades are coming.*
Allah, bring the blades. Bring the men
swinging them. Bring the acid. Bring

the old gods & the new, the dragons
& the white walkers. Bring me a thousand
winters & a thousand summers. Bring me
what some prophecy or horoscope or wayward

fortune teller promised me. Bring something
more than just the stories of who've left us
& the ghosts who tell them.

Fatimah Asghar

Oh, Daughter

We're returning to Cambodia together, father and daughter,
and he walks away from the wide Prek Eng road,
          me rolling the black suitcase, chin down.
                    There are so many ways I bring him shame.
     Sitting with my legs crossed. Stomping as I walk.
               I know my foreignness in his country: when I fall off the bus
and I pretend the dirt is nothing on my knees,
          the rocks stuck to my hands
     cheap jewels that shake off as glitter, and he
he is behind me watching his step, grunting
               You embarrass me.

               Or we visit Angkor Wat and he tells me
     You get in for free being goan Khmer,
          but don't open your mouth.
                    When we get to the Bayon Tower, he tells me *You can't go.*
Your shorts are too short and you should have covered your legs.
     I don't open my mouth. But I should nod to everything he says
          or be in the kitchen
               helping my aunt gut the market fish.

The part in our trip where it's obvious
how American I am in the eyes of my Cambodian family: lips tight,
I roll my eyes at him and walk away as he speaks.
Bong Sota doesn't understand. She says, *You just like to get angry.*
Your father is a good father.
But there's no language to tell this cousin
how he makes me feel in my motherland.

I don't belong.
He's right, he's right. I knew it before, but now I believe him.
Embarrassing.

At dinner, he tries to apologize,
by giving me the biggest part of the fish, the pineapple in the soup, the tomato
my aunt has prepared by herself. He should be upset
when I remove them from my bowl
and toss them back in the soup.
Watch the fish go back to its bones, its scales, back
to the market and back to the sea. Everything goes
back to where it came. Not me.

We know the role of Cambodian daughters.
We know how diaspora works.

Oh daughter, you wouldn't like it here anyway.
Oh, goan srey, goan srey, goan srey.
If he leaves a green coconut for me sitting overnight
we know inside, the fruit flies will nest
and last one day.

Monica Sok

Refugees

They have no need of our help
So do not tell me
These haggard faces could belong to you or me
Should life have dealt a different hand
We need to see them for who they really are
Chancers and scroungers
Layabouts and loungers
With bombs up their sleeves
Cut-throats and thieves
They are not
Welcome here
We should make them
Go back to where they came from
They cannot
Share our food
Share our homes
Share our countries
Instead let us

Build a wall to keep them out
It is not okay to say
These are people just like us
A place should only belong to those who are born there
Do not be so stupid to think that
The world can be looked at another way

(Now read from bottom to top)

Brian Bilston

Home

Have I forgotten it—
wild conch-shell dialect,

black apostrophe curled
tight on my tongue?

Or how the Spanish built walls
of broken glass to keep me out

but the Doctor Bird kept chasing
and raking me in: This place

is your place, wreathed in red
Sargassum, ancient driftwood

nursed on the pensive sea.
The ramshackle altar I visited

often, packed full with fish-skull,
bright with lignum vitae plumes:

Father, I have asked so many miracles
of it. To be patient and forgiving,

to be remade for you in some
small wonder. And what a joy

to still believe in anything.
My diction now as straight

as my hair; that stranger we've
long stopped searching for.

But if somehow our half-sunken
hearts could answer, I would cup

my mouth in warm bowls
over the earth, and kiss the wet dirt

of home, taste Bogue-mud
and one long orange peel for skin.

I'd open my ear for sugar cane
and long stalks of gungo peas

to climb in. I'd swim the sea
still lapsing in a soldered frame,

the sea that again and again
calls out my name.

Safiya Sinclair

Undocumented Joy

I don't remember crossing

I can not tell you about the journey
sometimes I close my eyes
and imagine a pitch black sky
with a thousand little stars

imagine a poetic crossing

my Abuela's hand tugging at my arm
a rush of wind
Abuelo leading the way

I imagine crossing without fear
just dreams
and Abuela's goals
to raise my brother and me
into hardworking men

I crossed without the trauma
latching onto my body
crossed unscarred
even though
mis viejitos
tell me
how they had to
stuff the four of us under the backseat of a car

sometimes I wish I could remember
then maybe just maybe
I would have another story to tell

I can only tell you about how poor we were
living in that small apartment
in the Eastside
how embarrassed I was
to invite my friends over
even though we all lived like this

I can only tell you about how proud I was of Abuela
who asked me to teach her English
scribbled on the refrigerator door
You can sometimes see the residue
of the markers I used to teach her basic words
like thank you, god bless you & you are welcome

I wish you would ask of the memories
I had before my identity became political
about the laughs
the joy
the things I love
about the way we have managed to survive

I wish you would focus on the magic
that is to take this country's trash
and make it into art

I wish I could tell you about the journey
but all I know is that I am here

and I am not going anywhere
this is my home

now.

Yosimar Reyes

self-portrait with no flag

i pledge allegiance to my
homies   to my mother's
small & cool palms   to
the gap between my brother's
two front teeth   & to
my grandmother's good brown
hands   good strong brown
hands gathering my bare feet
in her lap

i pledge allegiance   to the
group text   i pledge allegiance
to laughter & to all the boys
i have a crush on   i pledge
allegiance to my spearmint plant
to my split ends   to my grandfather's
brain & gray left eye

i come from two failed countries
& i give them back   i pledge
allegiance to no land   no border
cut by force to draw blood   i pledge

allegiance to no government   no
collection of white men carving up
the map with their pens

i choose the table at the waffle house
with all my loved ones crowded
into the booth   i choose the shining
dark of our faces through a thin sheet
of smoke   glowing dark of our faces
slick under layers of sweat   i choose
the world we make with our living
refusing to be unmade by what surrounds
us   i choose us gathered at the lakeside
the light glinting off the water & our
laughing teeth   & along the living
dark of our hair   & this is my only country

Safia Elhillo

Afterword

A T THE LOWEST point on earth, Leymah Gbowee addressed us all. Speaking at the 2018 Nobel Laureates and Leaders Summit for Children, held along the Dead Sea, she told us about her first bed in a refugee camp in the '90s. How her mom stitched it together with things she'd gathered, and how, years later, Leymah became a Nobel Peace Prize winner for her work ending the war in Liberia. She said something we've all struggled to articulate in our lives, that "being a refugee is just a phase in your life" and that it too will pass.

The strangest thing about universal struggle is that at any moment, you can feel as if you're standing on the outside of your own life and looking in. This is what I felt when Leymah said those words. This is what I feel now. It was transformative; we were all crying, everyone for different reasons—me, because I believed her.

In that room of refugees, former refugees, and world leaders fighting to end child labor and trafficking, I believed that we would become more than the threat of our histories. That we would be triumphant in the face of adversity because we'd fight for it, and we wouldn't stop until our voices were heard. The next day I started my mission with the UN Refugee Agency in Jordan, and one month after that, I got the invitation to contribute to *Ink Knows No Borders*.

I didn't hesitate to say yes. The timing was impeccable, the heart of the collection so relevant, and the people so invested in each individual message. Later, when I heard that the idea for this collection started more than a decade ago, I wasn't surprised. There were so many times growing up when I'd wished to find something like this, language to validate the struggle of existing in the middle, of being a third culture kid from war or otherwise and yet making it through to transform the lives we'd been given.

It isn't always pretty, and it isn't always successful, the people we've lost along the way are a testament to that, but it's something universal, something impossible to deny—people are going through this every day. I'm twenty-four as I write this, and by the time you read these words, I will be the age my mother was when she had to leave home and never look back. I can't imagine leaving now, I can't imagine picking up and starting over without any promise of tomorrow, not at this age, not at any other; but I know we didn't have another choice.

Poetry put choice back in my hands. It made it easier to mourn, to explore, and to recognize the realities I'd come from, the ones I passed through, and the new identities I'm discovering every single day. It means a lot to be in these pages, and it means even more to know that these words might move someone, to triumph, to act, to influence. My baby sister will turn two years old by the time this book is out. It's comforting to know that she will read this one day and understand what it means to be us.

Being a refugee is a phase, but being an advocate for change, that's something we should all be in every walk of life, in every country, in every place. You don't have to go on UN missions, travel across borders, or fight for children's rights to make a difference. You just have to reach out and recognize people. Recognize our fellow humans around the world who are fighting for the right to exist. Be an advocate for each other. This is why I fight for refugees, and this is why I write, because the simplest and deepest way to stand in solidarity with someone is to recognize them.

The poets in this book have fought to be heard, not only by beating adversity, but by being the very best at what they do, and in some cases, by being the very first to do it. We've grown up to be the writers we'd wished for as children, and we're striving to be the role models we'd looked up to in our youth. Our words are a testament to everything we've been through as children of diaspora and everything we've achieved as wielders of the pen. But the struggle won't be done until we're united in lifting the most unheard voices.

Acknowledge the pain, acknowledge the peace, acknowledge the love there is, and acknowledge the privilege that exists in reading what others have lived. The poets collected here have brought their voices forward. The rest is up to you.

EMTITHAL MAHMOUD

Acknowledgments

Because we are a country of immigrants, poets, and readers, there has always been a need for a book such as this, if only to recognize and celebrate who we are as a nation. Many years ago, Patrice envisioned creating such a book, and she invited Alyssa to edit it with her. She mulled on the idea, but there wasn't a sense of urgency. All that changed with the 2016 presidential campaign and the election of Donald Trump.

We are proud and honored to be able to include the work of sixty-four terrific poets in *Ink Knows No Borders*, and we are grateful that they are sharing their poems with the world. In particular, we would like to thank Javier Zamora for his foreword and Emtithal Mahmoud for her afterword. We also thank Eavan Boland for easing the way.

Not only is home essential for people's welfare, but without a publisher, a book remains homeless. We are thrilled with the home that *Ink Knows No Borders* has found with Seven Stories Press! Many thanks to Dan Simon, Ruth Weiner, Lauren Hooker, Anastasia Damaskou, Abigail Miller, and Stewart Cauley.

Without our agent Charlotte Cecil Raymond, whose belief in our book is boundary-less, we'd have never found our home at Seven Stories. With *Ink Knows No Borders*, Charlotte has gone above and beyond her duties, and we are enormously grateful for the scope of her vision and her sleuth-like work in finding hidden poems and poets. Patrice is grateful to Charlotte for being her dedicated agent over many years.

Additionally, Patrice thanks her husband Michael, once again, for his support of this book, and the love that he's given her and her books over the last couple of decades. Because of him, not only her books but everything in her world is better. Patrice also gives thanks to that natural world around her home that accepts her presence on miles of trails, time and time again, giving her the beautiful illusion that the world is borderless. Patrice's grandfather, Pasquale Vecchione, was a young man when he left his small village in Southern Italy to forge a new life in the United States, far from family. He arrived at Ellis Island without much and made a home in Brooklyn, becoming an electrician and a wrought-iron worker. Her thanks is decades late but, Grandpa, here it is. Alyssa Raymond's smarts, her knowledge of poets and poetry, her sensitive ear, and her hard work have made her the perfect co-editor of *Ink Knows No Borders*.

Alyssa thanks her family (Team Raymond) and her friends for all of their love and support, and she is grateful to Patrice Vecchione for her encouragement over the years and for giving her the opportunity to collaborate on this extraordinary collection.

Biographies

National Poetry Slam champion **Elizabeth Acevedo** is the *New York Times* bestselling author of *The Poet X*, the winner of the National Book Award, among other works of fiction and poetry. She's given TED Talks and has presented her work at such venues as Lincoln Center and the Kennedy Center, as well as farther afield in Kosovo, Brussels, and South Africa. The daughter of Dominican immigrants, her writing often reflects her Afro-Latina roots. On her website, Acevedo wrote, "I commit wholeheartedly to the mission that my mother's stories will not die with her. I believe wholeheartedly telling my own story is an act of love and survival." About her poem "Atlantis," she says, "[It] was inspired by the geography of the Dominican Republic and Haiti. When an island is already fighting over resources, what happens when those resources are even further threatened by climate change?" A New York City native, she now makes her home in Washington, DC. (acevedowrites.com)

Samira Ahmed is the *New York Times* bestselling author of the young adult novels *Love, Hate & Other Filters* and *Internment*. She was born in Bombay, India, and raised near Chicago, and her poetry and fiction often draw upon her own encounters with racism and hate crimes. About her poem "On Being American," she says, "[It was] inspired by my first experience with Islamophobia during the Iran Hostage Crisis. That's when I first learned that words could be daggers. But I also learned that words can be a balm; they can give us hope; they can let us breathe. And they can voice our resistance." After receiving her MAT from the University of Chicago, she taught high school English and worked for educational nonprofits, helping to create small high schools in New York City. (samiraahmed.com)

An Iranian American poet, editor, and professor, **Kaveh Akbar** is the author of the highly acclaimed poetry collection *Calling a Wolf a Wolf* and the founder of *Divedapper*, which features interviews with many of today's prominent poets. Born in Tehran, he was two when his family immigrated to the US. Prayer was a part of his upbringing, and though Akbar didn't yet understand Arabic he was fascinated by the ritual. In "Kaveh Akbar: How I Found Poetry in Childhood Prayer," published by *Literary Hub*, he wrote, "I remember watching my father, the only one of us who was actually raised entirely in Iran, who seemed specifically marked, fluid, holy in these moments. Before I really even understood the point of the praying, I understood that I wanted to be like him—['Learning to Pray'] orbits that idea." (kavehakbar.com)

When **Francisco X. Alarcón** was a teenager, poetic inspiration came to him through the songs his grandmother sang, and he went on to become a prolific writer for adults as well as children. Born in California and raised in Mexico, he returned to the US for college and graduate school. Not only fluent in English and Spanish, he also spoke Nahuatl, the language of the Aztecs. His poetry books include *Body in Flames/Cuerpo en llamas* and *Snake Poems: An Aztec Invocation*, winner of the American Book Award from the Before Columbus Foundation. About his poem "I Used to Be Much Much Darker," he said, "After spending a few months at Stanford University studying as a graduate student, I went home to visit my family in Southern California. Upon seeing me, Mother asked me what had happened to me since I had lost my dark-color complexion. I was really taken by her question, and noticed that, in fact, I was not as 'dark' as I used to be." Alarcón died in 2016.

An award-winning Palestinian American poet, novelist, and clinical psychologist, **Hala Alyan** is the author of the poetry collections *Atrium*, *Four Cities*, *Hijra*, and *The Twenty-Ninth Year*, as well as the novel *Salt Houses*. Born in Illinois, she grew up in various parts of the US and in Kuwait, Lebanon, Syria, and the United Arab Emirates. When her family sought asylum in Oklahoma after Saddam Hussein's invasion of Kuwait, she was five and didn't speak English; her poem "Oklahoma" reflects many of her struggles to fit in, when she felt like she didn't belong anywhere. "I was neither white nor Black nor Mexican, which meant, in the topography of my public elementary school in Oklahoma, that I was landless," she wrote in *Lenny Letter*. "I had multiple rituals, verging on the obsessive-compulsive" to "keep the funnel clouds from touching down" and "studied the clouds outside not for faces but for threats." (halaalyan.com)

Fatimah Asghar is a nationally touring poet, screenwriter, educator, performer, and writer/co-creator of *Brown Girls*. She is the author of the poetry collections *After* and *If They Come for Us*, as well as the co-editor, with Safia Elhillo, of the anthology *Halal If You Hear Me*. She was born in Massachusetts to Pakistani and Kashmiri immigrant parents who died when she was five, and many of her poems are about the trauma of loss. "Being a part of any kind of diaspora is such a beautifully haunting and strange experience, to kind of constantly be working back toward a place where your family has left, or were exiled from, or can't go back to . . . That's a kind of orphaning in its own self," she told *PBS NewsHour*. Her writing "came from a really dark place," but it is also about "having lived through that kind of darkness" and "having been able to construct [poetry] out of trauma . . . I write for the people who come before me and the people who might come after, so that I can honor them and create space for what is to come," she said in a *Prairie Schooner* interview. (fatimahasghar.com)

JoAnn Balingit is a poet, educator, arts-in-education advocate, and editor, as well as a surfer who rides a nine-foot-two longboard. A former poet laureate of Delaware, she is a Poetry Out Loud program coordinator and the author of three poetry collections, including, most recently, *Words for House Story*. She was born in Ohio to a German American mother and a Filipino immigrant father, and she grew up in Florida, the third eldest in a family of twelve children. About her poem "#Sanctuary," she says, "The day after the 2016 presidential election, I returned to teach at the local high school where I was a visiting poet. Some undocumented students left school that day, upset by a teacher who echoed the president-elect's August 2016 campaign speech on immigration: 'We will end the sanctuary cities that have resulted in so many needless deaths . . .' I wanted to write a poem for those students, to acknowledge their fear and courage." (joannbalingit.org)

Ellen Bass is a chancellor of the Academy of American Poets, whose most recent poetry collection, *Like a Beggar*, was a finalist for several awards, including the Lambda Literary Award and the Northern California Book Award. She co-edited the first major anthology of twentieth-century American women's poetry, *No More Masks!*, and co-authored *The Courage to Heal: A Guide for Women Survivors of Child Sexual Abuse*. Her father was born in Russia and came to the US as a child; her mother's parents emigrated from Lithuania. About writing "Ode to the Heart," she says, "My father's story is one that he told a number of times when I was a child. Anti-Semitism and tribalism were facts of life for my parents. In this poem, I tried to inhabit my father's boyhood experience through the heart that is common to all of us." (ellenbass.com)

Pseudonymous English author **Brian Bilston** has been described as "the Poet Laureate of Twitter." His 2016 collection, *You Took the Last Bus Home*, features many of the poems he's shared on social media, and his debut diary-style novel, *Diary of a Somebody*, combining poetry and fiction, follows his decision "to write a poem every day for a year." About his poem "Refugees," which can be read from beginning to end as well as from its last line to its first, Bilston says, "I was struck by how polarized the debates over the refugee crisis had become—how could these tragic stories of displacement, these poor people forced from their homes by war, famine and poverty elicit such diametrically opposed reactions from the rest of the world? I wanted to represent this contrast in a poem somehow. My own sympathies lie very much from the bottom upwards." (brianbilston.com)

Born in Ireland, **Eavan Boland** is regarded as an Irish poet, even though she has lived much of her life in the US. The author of nearly twenty poetry collections, as well as prose, including *Object Lessons: The Life of the Woman and the Poet in Our Time*, she is the director of Stanford University's creative writing program, a member of the Irish Arts Council and the Irish Academy of Letters, and a recipient of the Lannan Award for Poetry and an American Ireland Fund Literary Award. About her beginnings as a poet, Boland said in an interview with HoCoPoLitSo's *The Writer's Voice*, "Every young poet . . . goes through a stage of writing somebody else's poem . . . Fundamentally, if you learn to write someone else's poem, it will end up suppressing your own voice." (creativewriting.stanford.edu/people/eavan-boland)

Marci Calabretta Cancio-Bello was born in South Korea and adopted as a baby by a family in upstate New York. About her poem "Origin/Adoption," she says, "It's strange to wonder what cultural and genetic memories I might carry in my unconscious, and what permissions and rights I have to claim either South Korean or American cultures. [This poem] is a way of trying to talk about that experience and offer solidarity through the complexities of adoption that only other adoptees can recognize." Cancio-Bello has received poetry fellowships from Kundiman, the Knight Foundation, and the American Translators Association. Her debut poetry collection, *Hour of the Ox*, won an AWP Donald Hall Prize for Poetry. (marcicalabretta.com)

Poet, essayist, translator, and immigration advocate **Marcelo Hernandez Castillo** is the author of the poetry collections *Cenzontle* and *Dulce*, as well as a memoir. When he was five he crossed the US–Mexico border with his family, settling in California, and he was the first undocumented student to earn an MFA at the University of Michigan. He is also a founding member of the Undocupoets campaign. In an interview with *PBS NewsHour*, he said, "[Prior to becoming a DACA student] I couldn't bring myself to talk about being undocumented, what it's like . . . being a second grader and . . . worrying about state tests, if they ask for a social [security number]." About writing "Field Guide Ending in a Deportation," a direct response to Trump's immigration policies and anti-immigrant rhetoric, he told the *New York Times*, "Now, I feel like I'm giving myself permission . . . Am I enough? When is it going to be enough? . . . When I came undocumented into this country, I wanted to learn English so that I could be considered 'enough.' But after this terrible year, it's been solidified in me that maybe, that'll never be reached. It's a very sad poem." (marcelohernandezcastillo.com)

Marianne Chan, a writer of both poetry and fiction, grew up in Germany and Michigan, and now lives in Florida. She is the poetry editor at *Split Lip Magazine* and the author of the poetry collection *all heathens*. About "When the Man at the Party Said He Wanted to Own a Filipino," Chan says, "When I wrote this poem, I was reading *Magellan's Voyage Around the World*, which chronicles the 'discovery' of the Philippines by Ferdinand Magellan. This book and the conversation with the man at the party made me think about all the ways in history and in present times that Filipinos have been viewed as something that could be 'owned'—whether in marriage, as domestic workers, as outsourced labor, or, in the 1500s, as a 'heathen' people with resources that could be sold." (https://www.mariannechan.com)

The author of the poetry chapbook *Past Lives, Future Bodies*, **Kristin Chang** is the recipient of a Pushcart Prize in poetry and was a Gregory Djanikian Scholar. She says, "The concept of 'Domesticity' reflects not only what it means to be objectified as an 'other,' but also explores how immigrant women's and women of color's domestic labor is often invisibilized. I wrote this poem as a way of deconstructing the foreign/domestic and masculine-public versus feminine-domestic dichotomies that often erase the stories and voices of immigrant women." (kristinchang.com)

Leila Chatti is a Tunisian American dual citizen and the author of the poetry collections *Ebb* and *Tunsiya/Amrikiya*. In 2017, she was the first

North African poet to be shortlisted for the Brunel International African Poetry Prize. Many of her poems explore her own experiences of having two cultures, languages (Arabic and English), and faiths (Muslim and Catholic). "I was eleven years old when the Twin Towers fell and so came of age in the context of a country that despised me . . . That sense of being 'bad' and an outsider rooted in me," she told *Adroit Journal*. "*Tunsiya/Amrikiya* arose naturally, out of necessity. 2016 was a brutal, terrifying year to be Arab and Muslim in the United States . . . I like to think that these poems may . . . push back against Islamophobia, though they are not explicitly political; hatred is often the failure to see a stranger as fully human, and in these poems I reveal my full self." (leilachatti.com)

Cathy Linh Che is a Vietnamese American poet from Los Angeles, whose parents' stories about the Vietnam War inspired her award-winning debut poetry collection, *Split*. "My parents . . . clandestinely escaped on a boat soon after the fall of Saigon in 1975 . . . my mom told me she had no choice but to leave," she told the *Best American Poetry APIA Series*. "So, who am I? I am my family and my family's stories . . . I am my father who was drafted into the South Vietnamese Army and fought, an unwilling soldier, for over twelve years. I am my father's brother and aunt's children who were gunned down in one great massacre. I am my grandmother's grief, and also her endurance . . . I am also a girl who was sexually molested repeatedly over the course of eight years . . . I hope that putting my writing out there can help others feel less alone." (@cathylinhche)

Chen Chen, who was born in Xiamen, China, and grew up in Massachusetts, is the author of *When I Grow Up I Want to Be a List of Further Possibilities*, which received multiple honors and accolades. He is the 2018–2020 Jacob Ziskind Poet-in-Residence at Brandeis University, and co-edits the *Underblong*. About his poem "First Light," featured as part of the #WeComeFromEverything campaign, he wrote on his website, "I'm tired of the dominant immigration narrative, the one that romanticizes the United States as a land of opportunity and fails to recognize the deep sorrow many immigrants confront, leaving a home country—even when it's a real choice to do so. I'm also tired of what has more recently become the dominant coming-out narrative, the happy tale of full acceptance that marginalizes the experiences of those who aren't so fortunate to have supportive family. This poem is an attempt to hold heartbreak close." (chenchenwrites.com)

Franny Choi is a Korean American poet, playwright, teacher, and National Poetry Slam finalist, whose poetry collections include *Floating, Brilliant, Gone, Death by Sex Machine,* and *Soft Science.* She's a Kundiman Fellow, senior news editor for *Hyphen,* co-host of the podcast *VS,* and a member of the Dark Noise Collective. Her poem "Choi Jeong Min," which was written in response to a white poet who gained notoriety for using an Asian pseudonym, is about her own struggles to accept her identity as the daughter of Korean immigrants. In an interview with *Adroit Journal,* she said, "I grew up thinking it was one of my greatest strengths to not have a Korean accent; I even remember studying the speech patterns of other Korean-American kids so I wouldn't sound like them . . . I know that in some ways, no matter how perfect my English is . . . I'll always be seen as someone doing, at best, an extraordinarily good job at emulating a native speaker. But I think it's a beautiful gift to have grown up with the understanding that all English is broken; all English is breakable. I have no respect for the sanctity of English." (frannychoi.com)

Jeff Coomer, the author of *A Potentially Quite Remarkable Thursday,* grew up in the suburbs east of Baltimore. After working for many years in the corporate world, he completed training to be a Tree Steward. About "History Lesson," he says, "The statement my grandfather made that ends the poem was such a powerful reminder of the difference between his life of struggle and my life of privilege that I could still recall the details of the conversation when I wrote the poem more than thirty years later. I like to think his words made me a more sensitive and humble person as I moved into the adult world of work and family." (http://www.facebook.com/jeff.coomer.3)

Eduardo C. Corral is the author of the poetry collections *Slow Lightning*, which won the Yale Younger Poets Prize in 2012, making him the award's first Latino recipient, and *Guillotine*. The son of Mexican immigrants who crossed into Arizona shortly before he was born, he told *PBS NewsHour* that he hopes his poems will convey what he believes is largely missing from the national conversation about immigrants: "We keep seeing immigrants from Mexico, Central America, as labor force. [We] see them as . . . just physical beings, right? No! Everybody has a mind, a heart, a soul . . . [T]he cerebral, the mental, the emotional . . . gets often lost when we talk about immigration . . .There are days when [I'm] like, 'What am I doing at the desk? . . . I should be doing something to really mobilize . . . But we do need poets . . . from these kinds of backgrounds, Mexican-Americans, from El Salvador, from Guatemala, telling these stories." (@eduardoccorral)

Blas Manuel De Luna was born in Tijuana, Mexico, and was raised in California. His poetry collection *Bent to the Earth* reflects on his experiences working in the agricultural fields while he was growing up, and it was selected as a National Book Critics Circle finalist in 2006. In a profile in *Poetry*, he said, "I'm not by nature the kind of person who reveals himself, but it just kind of happens in the poems—the willingness to go to the place where you're revealed, but always in service of the poem, never in a purging kind of way." (blasmanueldeluna.com)

Safia Elhillo, who once carried a sign at a rally that read "Unapologetic Black Muslim Sudanese American (This Is My Country Too)," has found it difficult to know where she belongs, when her country of birth hasn't welcomed (and previously banned) her Sudanese family, and she didn't grow up in Sudan. "[If] my place of origin isn't home, and my place of birth isn't home, then what am I supposed to do? Where am I supposed to go? . . . My work has always come out of that space of questioning and discomfort," she told *Ploughshares*. Her poems reflect not only her own experiences of displacement and partial belonging, but that of her Sudanese parents', and of her grandfather's generation, born in Sudan under the British occupation. Her poetry collection *The January Children*, which was awarded the Sillerman First Book Prize for African Poets, is dedicated to these "January Children" who were assigned birth years by height and all given the birth date January 1. A recipient of the 2018 Ruth Lilly and Dorothy Sargent Rosenberg Poetry Fellowship, Elhillo is co-editor, with Fatimah Asghar, of the anthology *Halal If You Hear Me*. (safia-mafia.com)

As a poet, editor, essayist, and translator, **Martín Espada** has published almost twenty books, including, among his fourteen poetry collections, the Pulitzer Prize finalist *The Republic of Poetry*. His groundbreaking book of essays, *Zapata's Disciple*, which advocates for social justice, was once banned in Tucson as part of the Mexican American Studies Program outlawed by the state of Arizona. Espada's aim, he told Bill Moyers in an interview, has always been "to speak on behalf of those without an opportunity to be heard." Political activism is in his blood—his father, Frank Espada, was an acclaimed political activist and documentary photographer who emigrated from Puerto Rico to New York City. In an interview with *PBS NewsHour*, he said, "To see dignity in those faces where others did not see dignity, to recognize that our struggle as a community was and continues to be a struggle between dignity and indignity, between humanity and dehumanization. That's what you can do if you're a photographer or a poet." Formerly a tenant lawyer for Greater Boston's Latino community, Espada is a professor of English at the University of Massachusetts Amherst. He is the recipient of numerous awards, including the 2018 Ruth Lilly Poetry Prize. (martinespada.net)

Tarfia Faizullah is the author of the poetry collections *Seam* and *Registers of Illuminated Villages*. She has been honored with three Pushcart Prizes. In 2016, Faizullah was recognized by Harvard Law School as one of "50 Women Inspiring Change." Her poem "Acolyte" captures her own childhood experience. In an interview with *Grist Journal*, she said, "I grew up in West Texas in a Bangladeshi Muslim household in which Bangla was the primary language spoken. In the evenings, we prayed Maghrib and ate rice and lentils with our (right) hands, and in the mornings, I would wake up and go to the Episcopalian private school and attend the daily chapel service . . . Each time I went to Bangladesh, it was impossible to convey to my cousins what it was like to be an acolyte. Language has always been a way for me to try to articulate the strange and familiar wonder of both returning to Bangladesh and returning to Texas: those places that are both and neither my homelands. I think there's such richness in the space between those worlds, even though some days I want to disavow them." Faizullah is the Nicholas Delbanco Visiting Professor in Poetry at the University of Michigan. (tfaizullah.com)

Poet, editor, and nonfiction writer **Hafizah Geter** was born in Nigeria and immigrated to the US with her family when she was a toddler. The daughter of a Nigerian mother from a Muslim family and an American father raised Southern Baptist in Alabama, her dual cultural heritage inspires much of her writing. In an interview with the *New York Times*, she said, "Often, people think that for an immigrant, the whole thing is just this big gift that you're receiving. Of course when you're leaving a place for a better life it's a gift, but it becomes such a big cost to the person that's leaving." Geter believes that the power of poetry is that it "cannot be controlled, and it's especially dangerous because it's a tool used in minority and disenfranchised communities. The very act of speaking up in a world that tries to silence you—especially when you're coming from a marginalized identity—can actually have life or death consequences." Geter is a Cave Canem Fellow and an editor at Amazon Publishing's Little A and Day One. She is at work on a poetry collection and a nonfiction book exploring the intersection of gender, nationality, race, and the human condition. (hafizahgeter.com)

Carlos Andrés Gómez is a "proud Colombiano poet from New York City." About poetry, he says, "Oftentimes the greatest writing is putting down on paper what you know you shouldn't write." In addition to defying any "should" on paper and with his performances at slams, this spoken-word poet has raised over $40,000 to fight HIV/AIDS. Gómez graduated with an MFA from Warren Wilson College. The author of the memoir *Man Up: Reimagining Modern Manhood*, he's the winner of the Lucille Clifton Poetry Prize and has twice been nominated for a Pushcart Prize, including for "Pronounced," a poem that, as he wrote on the *Crab Orchard Review* blog, was "inspired by my childhood: growing up feeling pulled between languages, identities, and worlds." Gómez has performed on HBO's *Def Poetry Jam* and had a leading role in Spike Lee's blockbuster film *Inside Man*. (carloslive.com)

Gabriella Gutiérrez y Muhs, a graduate of Stanford University, is a poet, the author of several books, and an academic. She is the first editor of the pathbreaking *Presumed Incompetent: The Intersections of Race and Class for Women in Academia*. In 2017 Gutiérrez y Muhs received the Award for Outstanding Scholarship in Arts and Sciences from Seattle University, where she is a professor. Her collections of poetry include *A Most Improbable Life* and *The Runaway Poems: A Manual of Love*. She wrote her poem "Las Casas Across Nations" in response to the ongoing US–Mexican border crisis, saying, "the border has always been a porous region," across which her family traveled back and forth for more than one hundred years. (seattleu.edu/artsci/about/faculty-and-staff/gabriella-gutierrez-y-muhs-phd.html)

Born in the Philippines, **Janine Joseph** immigrated to the US with her family when she was eight. It wasn't until she received her federal Student Aid Report during her senior year of high school that she learned she wasn't a citizen, which meant she had to turn down college acceptances and scholarships. Joseph is an active member of Undocupoets, a group that promotes the work of undocumented poets. About writing her debut collection of poems, *Driving Without a License*, which won the 2014 Kundiman Prize, she said, in an interview with the Asian Pacific American Librarians Association, "It was impossible for me to tell a straightforward, linear immigration narrative wherein I easily immigrated, overcame adversity, assimilated, and then achieved the American Dream. Poetry allowed me to approach my story a fragment at a time. More, though it had been a fairly private and personal art and undertaking when I was younger, poetry became a voice and vocation that required no one's permission or authorization but mine." She is currently an assistant professor of creative writing at Oklahoma State University. In addition to being a poet, Joseph is a librettist, and her work has been commissioned for the Houston Grand Opera. (janinejoseph.com)

Mohja Kahf was born in Syria and came to the US when she was three. A writer from childhood, she was first published when she was ten and won a poetry contest in high school. She has authored two books of poetry, *E-mails from Scheherazad* and *Hagar Poems*; a novel, *The Girl in the Tangerine Scarf*; and many works of nonfiction, including *Western Representations of the Muslim Woman: From Termagant to Odalisque*. In an interview for *Medium*, she said she is inspired by the "rich heritage of Arab foremothers in poetry, even if, yes, they're always pulling against how they get marginalized and condescended to." As a member of the Syrian Nonviolence movement, Kahf works to help Syrians in crisis and to educate Americans about the country of her birth. She told *Medium*: "I think that activism for human rights, including gender rights, has this built-in impetus that it wants to reach people. It means seeing people's language and people's stories as sources for your telling, as muses among your muses." She's a professor at the University of Arkansas. (@ProfKahf)

Ilya Kaminsky, who lost most of his hearing when he was four, was born in the former Soviet Union city of Odessa and came to the US as a teenager when his family was granted asylum. He began writing poems in English when his father died a year after their arrival. "I understood right away that it would be impossible for me to write about his death in the Russian language," he explained in an interview with the *Adirondack Review*. "I chose English because no one in my family or friends knew it—no one I spoke to could read what I wrote. I myself did not know the language. It was a parallel reality, an insanely beautiful freedom." His poetry collections *Dancing in Odessa* and *Deaf Republic* demonstrate his love of languages and the ways that they transform us. Once a law clerk for San Francisco Legal Aid and the National Immigration Law Center, Kaminsky currently works as a court-appointed special advocate for orphaned children and teaches English and comparative literature at San Diego State University. (ilyakaminsky.com)

Li-Young Lee was born in Indonesia to Chinese political exiles who had fled China's turmoil. Persecution followed the family to Indonesia, as well, where his father was charged with crimes against the state and imprisoned. While his family was being taken to a prison colony, they escaped, and were eventually able to obtain asylum in the US. His memoir, *The Winged Seed: A Remembrance*, centers around the upheaval of his early life. Lee's many poetry collections have received numerous awards and honors, including recognition from the National Endowment for the Arts and the Guggenheim Memorial Foundation. Through writing poetry as a university student, Lee found a way to make the English language his own. In an interview with *Image*, he said, "The whole enterprise of writing absolutely seems to me like a spiritual practice . . . When you practice an art form, you realize that the poem is a descendent of your psyche, but your psyche, if you pay attention, is a descendent of something else, let's say the cosmos."

Joseph O. Legaspi was born in the Philippines and his family immigrated to California when he was twelve. The author of the poetry collections *Imago*, *Threshold*, and several chapbooks, he received a poetry fellowship from the New York Foundation for the Arts and co-founded Kundiman, a nonprofit organization dedicated to nurturing writers and readers of Asian American literature. In an interview with the *Creative Independent*, Legaspi said, "My pursuing something creative leads to this amazing brotherhood and sisterhood and siblinghood with creative folks. That's the best thing about being a creative, because I would say 90% of your friends are creative. They, in turn, bring so much beauty and language and sunlight, and darkness, and drama in your life. You feel alive all the time, having all these people around you. I'm really thankful for it." (josepholegaspi.wordpress.com)

Ada Limón is the author of five books of poetry, including, most recently, *The Carrying*, as well as *Bright Dead Things*, which was a finalist for both the National Book Award in Poetry and the National Book Critics Circle Award, and was named one of the Top Ten Poetry Books of the Year by the *New York Times* in 2015. Describing her poetry as mostly autobiographical, she told an interviewer from *Compose*: "I want my poetry to help people recommit to the world we are living in, to the ugly mess and beautiful strangeness of it. I don't provide any answers in my poems, but I hope to ask the right questions and reveal the right truths that make people feel like they aren't alone. I've said before that the most important words, for me, in poems are the words that aren't written, the words that say, 'me too.'" Limón makes her home in Lexington, Kentucky, and is on the faculty of the Queens University of Charlotte low-residency MFA program and the 24Pearl Street online program for the Provincetown Fine Arts Work Center. (adalimon.com)

The author of the poetry collection *Sisters' Entrance*, **Emtithal Mahmoud** was born in Sudan and came to the US in 1998 as a child refugee. She won the 2015 Individual World Poetry Slam Championship with her poem "Mama." In an interview with *PRI's The World*, she said, "It's mostly about my mother on the surface, but the reality is that the things I learned from her she learned from her mother, and her mother before her . . . [I]t's about the women in my family, the women in my life." Since high school, she has been an activist dedicated to bringing attention to the violence in Darfur. "The interesting thing about war is that people seem to think there's a particular start and end to the war, but in reality, it's much messier than that. When Darfur was no longer on the front page of the *New York Times* every day, when people stopped talking about it in the big media outlets, people thought, 'Oh, the war must have stopped.' But the reality is, we're still living it every day," she told *PRI's The World*. Appointed a Goodwill Ambassador in 2018 for UNHCR, the UN Refugee Agency, she has traveled extensively to witness its work and has represented the organization at many high-profile events, including the Women's Forum for the Economy and Society. (@EmiThePoet)

Mia Ayumi Malhotra is a poet from the San Francisco Bay Area. The child of missionary parents, she moved with her family in 1990 to the Lao People's Democratic Republic, a country then coming out of Cold War isolation, a place without paved roads or traffic lights. It was there Malhotra began to write. In an essay for *Inheritance*, she recalled, "I wrote stories about the world around me, and when I didn't know the word for something, penciled in an empty speech bubble to indicate the presence of something that couldn't be articulated." Her debut poetry collection, *Isako Isako*, winner of the 2017 Alice James Award, follows four generations of female Japanese Americans, including an internment camp survivor, to explore how mass displacement and rampant racism in America's past relate to current events. A Pushcart nominee, she's received fellowships from the VONA/Voices Writing Workshop and Kundiman. (miamalhotra.com)

Rajiv Mohabir is a Guyanese American poet and translator of Indo-Caribbean origin. His parents emigrated from Guyana to London to Canada to New York City and then moved to Florida. During a difficult adolescence, Mohabir found solace in writing. He's the author of the poetry collections *The Taxidermist's Cut*, a Lambda Literary Award finalist, and *The Cowherd's Son*, winner of the Kundiman Prize. He describes his project *Coolitude: Poetics of the Indian Labor Diaspora* as "the cultural productions of writers, artists, musicians, and filmmakers who descend from indentured laborers ['coolies'] from Guyana, Trinidad, Suriname, Mauritius, South Africa, Fiji, and those in second diaspora in England, the United States, and Canada." In an essay for *Jacket2*, he wrote: "I am haunted by transoceanic crossings, the suppression of my familial religions and languages, and being thingified—albeit to a lesser extent than Black folks. This rich and colorful history shows up in my poetry as I write." Mohabir received his PhD in English from the University of Hawaiʻi and is currently an assistant professor of poetry at Auburn University. (rajivmohabir.com)

Born in Haiti and raised in the Boston suburbs, **Lenelle Moïse** is a poet, playwright, and performance artist who creates jazz-infused, hip-hop bred, politicized texts about the intersection of identity, memory, and spirit. In an interview with *Time Out New York*, Moïse said this about her performance work: "I'm really interested in breaking down the fourth wall of theater. And one of the ways is just by saying, 'I can hear you, I can see you. We're all in this together,' and trying to create a casual ceremony with the audience." Her performances include: *Where There Are Voices*, a response to the 2010 earthquake in Haiti based on her poetry collection *Haiti Glass*; *Speaking Intersections*, a queer feminist blend of poetry and prose; *Word Life*, an autobiographical coming-of-age story; and *K-I-S-S-I-N-G*, about teens bonding across their socioeconomic differences. In an interview with the Smith College alumnae magazine, she said, "I see poetry everywhere: in movement, in dialogue, in Haiti, in paintings, in the public-housing tenements of my memories, in embraces. My credo is that a poem is only effective on stage when my writing is pulsing with life." (lenellemoise.com)

A daughter of Dominican immigrants, **Yesenia Montilla** is an Afro-Latina poet, translator, and educator who was born and raised in New York City. She received her MFA from Drew University in Poetry and Poetry in Translation and was a 2014 CantoMundo Fellow. Her poetry collection, *The Pink Box*, was longlisted for a PEN award. In an interview for the *Letras Latinas* blog, she reflected on her poem "The Day I Realized We Were Black": "It was one of the most painful poems to write and took me nearly two years to be able to read it aloud without crying. And that is poetry, when the truth in the poem turns you so delicate that you break, then you know you're risking everything on the page." (yeseniamontilla.com)

Gala Mukomolova is a Russian American poet, essayist, and artist living in New York City, who, under the name Galactic Rabbit, writes horoscopes and love notes for *NYLON*. A recipient of the 2016 "Discovery"/*Boston Review* poetry contest prize, she is the author of the poetry collections *One Above/One Below: Positions & Lamentations* and *Without Protection*. In her essay "Golubki, Golubchik," published in *The Crazy Wisdom Community Journal*, she wrote: "Between worlds, I had too much language and not enough, and because of this I was a child who rarely spoke from a place of want. To express want was a sign of weakness, and I trained myself around it." (galacticrabbit.com)

Born to a Filipina mother and a father from South India, **Aimee Nezhukumatathil** spoke of her childhood in an interview for *Divedapper*: "Growing up as one of the only Asian-Americans in most of my school always set me a little apart, always observing. But my parents fostered a sense of being grateful and amazed and wanting to always be curious about the world and its inhabitants so I never truly felt alone." That curiosity led her to write poetry that is often inspired by her love of nature and science. She's the author of four poetry collections, most recently *Oceanic*, as well as *World of Wonder*, a book of illustrated nature essays. The Tupelo Press Prize, the Global Filipino Award, a Pushcart, and a National Endowment are among her distinctions. She teaches creative writing and environmental literature at the University of Mississippi and is the poetry editor of *Orion* magazine. In her *Divedapper* interview, she also said, "I'm not sorry for writing about wonder and joy." (aimeenez.net)

Hieu Minh Nguyen identifies himself as "a queer Vietnamese American poet and performer based out of Minneapolis." He's the author of the poetry collections *This Way to the Sugar*, which was a finalist for the Lambda Literary Award, and *Note Here*. He has received a 2018 Ruth

Lilly and Dorothy Sargent Rosenberg Poetry Fellowship, as well as fellowships from the NEA and Kundiman. He is also a poetry editor for *Muzzle Magazine* and an MFA candidate at Warren Wilson College. In an interview for *Poets & Writers*, he said, "For a long time, I didn't know how to write about my traumas. I found myself writing the same poems over and over again, even if they didn't make any sense to the world . . . I guess the hope was that if I could write the poems, if I could speak about my trauma in a way that didn't seem careless, I could stop trying to explain myself." (hieuminhnguyen.com)

The son of Mexican immigrants, **José Olivarez** is co-host of the podcast *The Poetry Gods* and the author of the poetry collection *Citizen Illegal*. He is a marketing manager for Young Chicago Authors (YCA), where he began writing poetry as a teen—an experience that helped prepare him for his admission to Harvard University. In an interview with the *Chicago Tribune*, he talked about overcoming the feelings of "weakness" he felt because of his native language and culture. "As I began writing, I realized I could be a part of a loving community. It didn't have to be me against the world; it was a community trying to build a new world for everyone we love." About his poem "ode to the first white girl i ever loved," Olivarez says, "I wrote [it] in a workshop while thinking about romantic love as a political choice. If I only see white women as beautiful, and I do not come from a white woman, then how do I see myself?" (joseolivarez.com)

Ladan Osman is a Somali-born American poet and educator whose work is centered on her Somali and Muslim heritage. She is the author of the poetry collections *Ordinary Heaven*, a chapbook which was included in *Seven New Generation African Poets*, a project of the African Poetry Book Fund, *The Kitchen-Dweller's Testimony*, which won the Sillerman First Book Prize for African Poets, and *Exiles of Eden*. A teacher by profession, she is also a contributing editor at the *Offing*. She grew up in a Columbus, Ohio, neighborhood that was largely populated by other East Africans, and she told the *Paris Review* that while she's "rooted to America," her "cellular memory calls to places I haven't seen in my adult life. Sometimes negotiating that feels like a challenge. In my poems, too—trying to figure out who the work is for, what the work is for, what it is meant to do." She added: "So many different elements go into my work, but there's a very direct link to the way my parents would tell stories—their comfort using parables, making leaps in language, speaking in metaphor." (@ OsmanLadan)

Craig Santos Perez is a native Chamoru (Chamorro) from the Pacific Island of Guåhan (Guam). As a poet, scholar, publisher, critic, artist, and environmental activist, he has co-edited three anthologies of Pacific Islander literature, and he has authored four poetry collections and two spoken word albums. In an interview for *NBC Asian America Presents: A to Z*, Perez said, "I am inspired by the ecology of the Pacific Islanders, the resilience of the Pacific Islanders, the wisdom of Pacific cultures, the brilliance of Pacific scholarship, and the beauty of Pacific arts," adding, "The forces of colonialism, militarism, and capitalism are challenges that impact all of us in the Pacific." About his poem "Off-Island Chamorros," he says it was "written to share my own migration story from Guam, a territory of the United States, and to provide context for the migration of my native Chamorro people." Perez teaches in the English department at the University of Hawaiʻi at Manoa. (craigsantosperez.com)

Spoken-word artist, poet, essayist, and activist **Bao Phi** was born in Vietnam and came to Minneapolis as a child with his family. He's a two-time Minnesota Grand Slam champion and a National Poetry Slam finalist, who has appeared on HBO's *Def Poetry Jam* and was featured in the award-winning documentary *The Listening Project*. His books include the poetry collections *Sông I Sing* and *Thousand Star Hotel*, as well as the picture book *A Different Pond*, which received a Caldecott Honor Award. BuzzFeed named *Thousand Star Hotel* one of the best poetry books of 2017, writing, "Bao Phi confronts the stereotype of being a 'model minority' . . . exploring Asian American poverty, racism and discrimination, police brutality, violence and trauma, identity, and fatherhood. Written with immense empathy and honesty, [it] is a moving, heartbreakingly beautiful portrait of the lives of Vietnamese refugees in the U.S." (baophi.com)

Poet, educator, and performance artist **Yosimar Reyes** was born in Mexico and came to California with his grandmother when he was three. In an interview with *Westword*, he said, "When I think of my culture, it is very American, but I lack the proper documentation to say that I'm an 'American,' whatever that means. Because I don't have a social security number and I lack access to a lot of things, I've found that art was something that was very accessible . . . Most of what I write focuses on intersections of migration and sexuality." He is the author of the poetry collection *for colored boys who speak softly* and artist-in-residence for *Define American*, the nonprofit media organization that fights injustice and anti-immigrant hate through the power of storytelling. Reyes is the co-founder of the performance ensemble La Maricolectiva, a community-based performance group of queer undocumented poets, which was featured in the award-winning documentary *2nd Verse: The Rebirth*. (yosimarreyes.com)

Alberto Ríos is a Mexican American poet from Nogales, Arizona. "My upbringing [near the Mexico–US border] was wonderful and I would not trade it for anything," he told an AARP VIVA interviewer. "It showed me how to look at everything in more than one way: different languages, different foods, different laws. The whole world was never simply one-dimensional. And for me as a writer—and later as a poet in particular—that was invaluable." Arizona's first poet laureate and an Academy of American Poets chancellor, Ríos is the author of ten books of poetry including, most recently, *A Small Story about the Sky*, as well as a memoir, *Capirotada*. (english.clas.asu.edu/content/alberto-rios)

Michelle Brittan Rosado is the author of the poetry collection *Why Can't It Be Tenderness*, which won the Felix Pollak Prize in Poetry. Her work appears in *Time You Let Me In: 25 Poets Under 25* and *Only Light Can Do That: 100 Post-Election Poems, Stories, & Essays*. Born in San Francisco, she's of mixed cultural heritage, including Malaysian on her mother's side. About her poem "Fluency," she says, "I wrote this poem thinking about the way immigration creates many kinds of distance in a family: not just geographical, but sometimes linguistically and emotionally. At the same time, it also strikes me as miraculous and beautiful that we find ways to bridge such spaces, however we can." Rosado is a Wallis Annenberg Endowed Fellow and PhD candidate in Creative Writing & Literature at the University of Southern California. (michellebrittanrosado.com)

Poet, novelist, and essayist **Erika L. Sánchez** is the daughter of undocumented Mexican immigrants and was raised outside of Chicago. She's received many fellowships and awards, including, most recently, a Princeton Arts Fellowship, and is the author of the poetry collection *Lessons of Expulsion* and the *New York Times* bestselling young adult novel *I Am Not Your Perfect Mexican Daughter*, which was a National Book Award finalist. "A ruthless reviser" is what she called herself in an interview for *RHINO*: "Usually, a poem begins as an image that gets stuck in my brain. I see or hear something grotesque or beautiful or both that startles me and then I become obsessed with it until it becomes a poem. Sometimes it takes me years to complete a poem. Sometimes they require me to leave them alone for months and months before I can revise them again . . . Poetry feels like my brain giving birth to something painful and grotesque." (erikalsanchez.com)

Solmaz Sharif was born in Istanbul as her parents made their way from their native Iran to the US several years after the 1979 Iranian Revolution. She is a poet who writes about the human costs of war and the political use of "insidious abuses against our everyday speech." Her first poetry collection, *LOOK*, was a National Book Award finalist. She has described her work as both "political" and "documentary," saying in an interview with the *Paris Review* that she has felt like an outsider despite growing up in a largely Iranian American community: "Aesthetics and politics have a really vital and exciting give-and-take between them . . . No matter where I went, I was outside of whatever community I found myself in, so that even when I arrived in a place where there was a lot of 'me,' I was totally outside again. That probably influenced my artistic impulse . . . to stand outside of and look into, and constantly question and interrogate the collectives that exist. It's easy for me because I've never felt a part of any of them in a real way." (solmazsharif.com)

Mahtem Shiferraw is a poet, short story writer, and visual artist from Ethiopia and Eritrea. Her poetry books include *Behind Walls & Glass*, *Fuchsia*, which received the Sillerman First Book Prize for African Poets, and *Your Body Is War*. She's the founder of Anaphora Literary Arts, a nonprofit organization working to advance the works of writers and artists of color, and co-founder of the Ethiopian Artist Collective. About her approach to writing, Shiferraw told the *Massachusetts Review*, "I see poems everywhere I go, whatever I'm doing. Sometimes it's a sound, or a color, or a perplexed expression. Sometimes poems come in the form of a character, or a conversation, and then they are shaped into prose (which eventually becomes part of my fiction writing). My job, besides listening to my characters, becomes then an act of mending of sorts; I patch poems here and there until I begin to acquire some clarity and make sense of a story, a plot line, a theme." (mahtem-shiferraw.com)

Terisa Siagatonu is a queer Samoan womyn poet, arts educator, and community organizer, who was born in the San Francisco Bay Area. In 2012, she received President Obama's Champion of Change Award for her activism as a spoken-word poet/organizer in her Pacific Islander community. When asked by the *Split This Rock* blog to recount a "proud poetry moment," Siagatonu replied, "Last year, I had the opportunity to visit American Samoa and spend an entire week leading writing workshops for 5 of the high schools on the island, including the one my father attended when he was a teenager . . . I've never felt so proud to be both Samoan and a writer. It meant everything to me to be able to share something as important as writing with my people, because both are the reasons why I'm still here and why I know who I am." (terisasiagatonu.com)

Safiya Sinclair was born and raised in Montego Bay, Jamaica. Her first full-length poetry collection, *Cannibal*, won the Prairie Schooner Book Prize in Poetry and the Phillis Wheatley Award, among many others. In a *PEN Ten* interview, she said, "It's hard to remember a time when 'writer' was really separate from my sense of identity—I began writing early at 10 or 11 and published my first work at 16 in Jamaica." Her first realization of what she wanted to write about came in college when she encountered overt racism: "And *that* was the moment I decided that my responsibility as a poet was to always keep my gaze centered on my Jamaican landscape, to tell the stories of Jamaican womanhood, of blackness and marginalization, to write against postcolonial history and nurture anti-colonial selfhood. To leave no space, no place, not even a sliver of consideration for the venal hegemony of whiteness in my imagination; dark, beautiful, and untamed." (safiyasinclair.com)

Cambodian American poet **Monica Sok** is the daughter of refugees and the granddaughter of Em Bun, a master silk weaver and NEA National Heritage Fellow. Her poetry collection *Year Zero* won the Poetry Society of America's Chapbook Fellowship, and she has received fellowships from the National Endowment of the Arts, Kundiman, and Stanford University, among others. About "Oh, Daughter," she says, "Writing this poem allowed me to process what 'belonging' means as a Cambodian American daughter. Falling short of both cultural and parental expectations, I am always aware of how others perceive shame. But the spirit of the poem is rooted in defying gendered expectations and embraces such agency." (@monicasokwrites)

Gary Soto was born to working-class parents in Fresno, California. While young, he worked in both the fields and factories. It was in high school that he became inspired to write after reading such authors as Hemingway, Frost, Wilder, and Steinbeck. "I was already thinking like a poet, already filling myself with literature," he recalled, in an interview with UC San Diego. Soto has published more than forty books for children, young adults, and adults, including most recently a new edition of his 1977 debut poetry collection, *The Elements of San Joaquin*, a pioneering work in Latino literature. The Gary Soto Literary Museum is located at Fresno City College. Of his job as a writer, he has said, "My duty is not to make people perfect, particularly Mexican Americans. I'm not a cheerleader. I'm one who provides portraits of people in the rush of life." (garysoto.com)

Filipino American poet **Jeff Tagami** was born and raised in California. When he was in his twenties, he joined the Kearny Street Workshop, an Asian American artists and writers' collective, publishing short stories and poems that focused on the struggles of factory and field workers, including *Without Names*, one of the first Filipino American poetry anthologies. He was featured reading his poem "Song of the Pajaro," about a day in the life of Pajaro Valley farmers, in the PBS film *The United States of Poetry*. Tagami died of cancer in 2012, and in an online remembrance, poet Alan Chong Lau said Tagami's poetry collection *October Light* "will go down in history as one of the classics of Filipino American literature . . . [It] is one of the first books that documents the history and lives of the rural Filipino and gives them a real voice."

Alice Tao was born in China in 1935. Due to Japan's invasion of China, her family was forced to move often over a period of several years. When they finally settled in a small village, Tao enjoyed a happy childhood in a safe environment, free to wander, picking berries by the river. Later, during the Chinese Civil War, her family fled to Hong Kong, her father certain that life as refugees was better than living under communism. Tao went to Taiwan for college, where she met her husband. From there they went to the United States. For many years, she taught Chinese at the Monterey

Institute of International Studies. Tao's love for poetry began when, as a small child, she sat beside her mother as she recited Tang Dynasty poems while rocking her baby sister to sleep.

Chrysanthemum Tran is a queer and transgender Vietnamese American poet, performer, and photographer, whose parents came to the US as refugees. A teaching artist for the Providence Poetry Slam youth team, she's the first transfeminine finalist at the Women of the World Poetry Slam, a Rustbelt Poetry Slam champion, and FEMS Poetry Slam champion, whom the Adobe Project 1324 named as one of their "5 Poets You Need to Follow Right Now." In an interview for the *Blueshift Journal,* she discussed how she became a poet: "When I was a little baby, when I was in public school in Oklahoma, the shit that changed my life was Maya Angelou. She was my first introduction to poetry that wasn't written by a cis white man or wasn't written in inaccessible language." (chrysanthemumtran.com)

Paul Tran is a Vietnamese American poet, slam poetry champion, educator, and editor who grew up in a San Diego neighborhood that included Vietnamese, Sudanese, Eritrean, and Mexican immigrants. "It's powerful," Tran said in an interview for *Northwest Asian Weekly,* "seeing refugees, immigrants, and families of color making sense of their new lives in the United States, its tragedies and triumphs, and exacting all their human gifts in the cultivation of futures that are, as many of us hope, brighter and safer than the futures we were once conferred. I saw this each time my mother swallowed the patronizing and racist and sexist ways her customers treated her, each time I took the bus two hours to and from high school . . . [where] wealth and conservatism told me I wasn't supposed to succeed in life or that I was inadequately built for the privileges others had." They are a 2018 Ruth Lilly and Dorothy Sargent Rosenberg Poetry Fellow, a poetry editor at the *Offing,* and a Chancellor's Graduate Fellow in the writing program at Washington University in St. Louis, Missouri. (iampaultran.com)

Lena Khalaf Tuffaha is an American poet, essayist, and translator of Palestinian, Jordanian, and Syrian heritage, who has lived and traveled throughout the Arab world. For many years, she volunteered for Seattle's Arab American community organizations to help people tell their stories of living between two homelands, and her poetry collections *Arab in Newsland* and *Water & Salt* are inspired by such experiences. In an interview for *Hedgebrook*, she said, "My mother's family is from Syria and Jordan. My father's family is from Palestine, and many of them became refugees after the 1967 war. My parents immigrated to the United States and I was born in Seattle. When I was three years old we moved back to the Arab world and I spent most of my childhood there. I grew up moving, moving back, travelling around a world I was introduced to as 'home.' In some ways, this is a quintessentially Arab experience. The tension between home and homeland, the transitory nature of belonging, these are themes that continue to interest me." (lenakhalaftuffaha.com)

Born in Saigon, **Ocean Vuong** immigrated to the US when he was two as a child refugee and grew up in Connecticut. The author of the multi-award-winning poetry collection *Night Sky with Exit Wounds* and the novel *On Earth We're Briefly Gorgeous,* he is an assistant professor in the MFA for Poets and Writers program at the University of Massachusetts Amherst. In an interview for *Divedapper*, he said, "I think my reckoning with the written word was also the reckoning with racism, which is sad, but also necessary and, in a way, a vital means of confronting the realities of my country, of America." As for the role of identity in his writing, he sees "[it] more as a thread being pushed through a piece of fabric as it's being woven, and that all of our identities are fibers woven in that thread. To write is to push all of oneself through that moment, through that space on the page. Of course, no matter what I do or say, I will always be an Asian-American, Vietnamese, Queer, etc., including all the identities that I don't even have the language for yet." (oceanvuong.com)

Award-winning Iranian-born poet and writer **Sholeh Wolpé** has authored four poetry collections and two plays, edited three anthologies, and translated four volumes of poetry, including, most recently, *The Conference of Birds* by Attar, the Sufi mystic poet. Her play *SHAME* was a 2016 Eugene O'Neill Theater Center's National Playwright conference semifinalist. In 2018 she was the inaugural Writer-in-Residence at UCLA. Born in Tehran, she spent her teen years in Trinidad and the UK before coming to the US. About her poem "Dear America," she says, "I kept going back to my journey towards America which in my young life was not a country but a dream space, somewhere out there, like music or a piece of art." (sholehwolpe.com)

Jenny Xie, who was born in China and raised in New Jersey, came to the US when she was four years old. Her debut poetry collection, *Eye Level*, won the Walt Whitman Award of the Academy of American Poets and Princeton University's Holmes National Poetry Prize and was a National Book Award finalist. When asked what advice she has for young writers, she told the blog *Speaking of Marvels*, "I'll echo what many poets have said . . . : read avidly and widely. There doesn't seem to be any substitute to that. You learn to internalize the rhythms of good writing through reading, and you sharpen your inner ear this way." Xie lives in Brooklyn and teaches at New York University. (jennymxie.com)

Javier Zamora was born in El Salvador and at the age of nine immigrated unaccompanied to the US through Guatemala, Mexico, and the Sonoran Desert. His poetry collection *Unaccompanied*, which won a Firecracker Award, explores the impact of migration and the Salvadoran Civil War on his family. He has been awarded numerous fellowships, including a Radcliffe Institute Fellowship and the Wallace Stegner Fellowship at Stanford University. About his poem "Second Attempt Crossing," Zamora says, "I wouldn't be here without the generosity, the humanity, of someone like Chino. Please acknowledge the humanity of humans that take a wrong path, especially now when Central Americans continue to be dehumanized by this government." (javierzamora.net)

Permissions

Index